Crapemyrtle

A Grower's Thoughts

by Marcus David Byers, Jr.

*"I have in it
communicated such notions
as I have gathered,
either from reading
of several authors,
or by conferring sometimes
with country people;
to which I have added
some observations of mine owne,
never before published:
Most of which I am
confident are true, and
if there be any that are not
so, yet they
are pleasant."*

William Coles, *The Art of Simpling (1656)*

The photo of the bark used on the cover is from Dr. J.C. Raulston, Raleigh, North Carolina
Inset front cover photo is Regal Red Crapemyrtle.
Inset inside front-cover photo is "Byers Wonderful White," photograph courtesy of Fleming's
Nurseries Pty. Ltd., Victoria, Australia.

Presented to
The
Fairhope Public Library

In Memory of

LOIS BERG

By

Alida Given
Linda Miller

August 2001

© 1997 Marcus David Byers, Jr.

Design by Ross Heck
Edited by George Littleton/Owl Bay Publishers

Published by Owl Bay Publishers, Inc.
Post Office Box 3592
Auburn, Alabama 36830

All photographs are from the collection of the author except where noted.

ISBN 1-885623-25-9

Manufactured in the United States of America

Using This Book

This book will help crapemyrtle users make intelligent and informed choices about creating beauty and easing maintenance responsibilities.

For too long, landscape professionals and gardeners have chosen to plant crapemyrtle only for the long-lasting and wonderfully colored flowers. This practice ignored opportunities created by the newest forms and features. Selecting the correct cultivar for a special spot eliminates unnecessary pruning and accomplishes the spectacular display imagined by the designer.

Here's how to use this book to make your way quickly through the information:

1. To find cultivars in a certain *color* see the chart on page 106; then, refer to the text for more details.

2. To find choices in a certain *height* see the chart on page 107; then, refer to the text for more details.

3. To read about a certain *cultivar*, see the chart on page 105, which will refer you to the proper page in the text.

4. Information on insects, diseases, pruning, winter hardiness, and general culture is in the text beginning on page 26. More specific page numbers will be found in the table of contents and index.

Contents

Thanks

I have loved putting this book together. As I wrote it I imagined I was talking with friends, and that visit made the writing easy. The audience for whom I have written includes:

- Nurserymen;

- Landscape architects and landscape contractors;

- Serious gardeners; and

- Students and others who want to know more about crapemyrtle.

It is unusual for a wholesale nurseryman to find the time for a project like this. Without the constant urging of those who saw the need, this book would never have been written.

My wife, Janie, traveled with me to many nurseries, gardens and libraries, put up with my wandering mind and cluttered notes and often saw a more clear path than I. As always, she was there when I needed her.

Marge Edde, my long time secretary, has for years made me look better than I am, especially on paper. She has proofed, corrected and improved letters, talks, articles and now this crapemyrtle book. I guess that I'm a lot like Bill Cosby's TV son, Theo, who often said, "I like to look good." Marge has seen to that for me. She has had a tough job.

Our many customers, who have paid the bills for years, have so often said, "You are the one to tell about crapemyrtle." They are in a large way responsible for this book. Their reactions, observations and comments rounded out my thoughts and led me to new areas of interest. These nurserymen made it possible for me to put my thoughts on paper.

It is risky to begin to list the many who have aided me; I am certain I will omit some. But I must chance that. Among them are George Bennett, a long-time friend and former partner; Harvey Cotten, executive director of the Huntsville Botanical Garden; Jeff Farmer of Walt Disney World Co.; Dr. Gary Knox of the University of Florida; at the National Arboretum, Ruth Dix and Dr. Margaret Pooler; and family members, Elizabeth Byers Herrin and Emily Steele Craft. Librarians Allison Levely at the Library of Congress, Jimmie Marshall of Columbiana, Alabama's Smith-Harrison Museum and Auburn University's Yvonne Kozlowski and Tom Glynn were wonderful.

Special thanks are due my son Marc Byers, whose energy was devoted to the nursery while I played at writing a book. And still he had time to read and suggest. Others are Dr. Mike Dirr, Nicholas Shields, Anne Andrick Stamper, Dr. Carl Whitcomb, Dr. Randy Johnson, Dr. John Pair, Professor Charles Korns, Don Shadow, Tommy Loder, Dean McLendon, Dr. Frank Philpot, Dr. Gary Keever, Ralph Pinkus, Dr. Govind Sharma and Dr. Al Einert.

Without the efforts of Dr. Donald Egolf, this book would be quite unnecessary. His intellectual abilities, quiet, competent manner, and diligent attention to detail are now evident in most southern gardens. His work extended far beyond the world of **Lagerstroemia**. We who love and enjoy nature's plants owe him a great debt.

My warmest thanks to all.

A Conversation About Crapemyrtle

Fantasy Crapemyrtle
(Photograph courtesy of Dr. J.C. Raulston, Raleigh, NC)

"Almost all landscape needs can be met by one of the various crapemyrtle."

Several Southern nurserymen recently pondered the question: "What is your favorite plant? Not the most profitable, but really your favorite?"

All struggled with their answers, because they think in terms of sales first. Dennis McCloskey mentioned his favorite had to be Live Oak, and gave good reasons for his choice. Don Shadow suggested his favorites were small flowering trees, such as **Cornus**, **Cladrastis**, **Halesia**, and crapemyrtle. Charles Elliott prefers Savannah Holly and Tom Dodd, Jr. likes most of the **Ilex** family. Frank Colvett chose **Ilex decidua**, Japanese Red Maple and Natchez crapemyrtle. Ronald Copeland answered as did I, crapemyrtle.

It only took me a moment to answer that query. I have always enjoyed the year-round beauty of these superb ornamentals. I have no doubt about my favorite.

There are many uses for this fascinating plant. In fact, almost all landscape needs can be met by one of the various crapemyrtle. They can serve as shade trees, large enough for a child's small swing, or a singing spot of color in the drab yard of a factory or warehouse.

The different shapes and colors allow crapemyrtle to be foundation or corner plants, hedges, screens, groundcover masses of eye-catching brightness, container gardens, small patio features, or street and highway plantings. Crapemyrtle can provide a streamer of summer brilliance leading the eye to the center of an auto sales lot, or stop traffic with carnival colors for fast food restaurants.

Crapemyrtle are easy to grow. Through the years, these wonderful and rugged plants have flourished in mild environments in many parts of the world. Literature from wide-ranging countries such as Iraq, Sri Lanka, Ceylon, Malaya, New Guinea, England, Philippines, India, China, Australia, Japan, and France indicates the varied regions where **Lagerstroemia** species are appreciated.

These wonderful and rugged plants have flourished in mild environments in many parts of the world.

The Lythraceae family includes about fifty species of **Lagerstroemia**. The most familiar are **Lagerstroemia indica**, **Lagerstroemia fauriei,** and hybrids of these two.

Several other species such as **Lagerstroemia subcostata**, **Lagerstroemia speciosa**, and **Lagerstroemia limii** may soon be included in hybridization efforts as attempts are made to extend the hardiness range, add or intensify flower colors, and eliminate insect and disease problems. For all practical purposes, limitations such as winter hardiness will continue to restrict their popularity to milder climates.

Crapemyrtle was an important plant in China before the time of recorded history. **Lagerstroemia** was described and illustrated in 1755 in a publication by a Dutch physician, G. H. Rumphius, who called them by the Chinese name "Tsjinkin." It was first planted and admired in the United States around 1750. During this period it was grown at the Kew Royal Botanic Gardens, near London, and in Charleston, South Carolina, and all along the eastern coast of the United States.

In 1759 Carl Linnaeus, the father of our orderly system of plant names, described and named **Lagerstroemia** in honor of his close friend, Magnus von Lagerstrom of Gothenberg, Sweden. Lagerstrom was an enthusiastic naturalist and worked with the Swedish East Indies Company, an early shipping business.

This Lagerstroemia indica, on the campus of the Mississippi College for Women in Columbus, is well over 50 years old.

Crapemyrtle was an important plant in China before the time of recorded history.

Linnaeus named Lagerstroemia in honor of his close friend, Magnus von Lagerstrom

George Washington, our first president, was quite a gardener—of necessity, since he was responsible for growing the food for the hundreds who worked at and visited his Mount Vernon estate. His writings often mentioned agricultural issues, such as this diary entry from 1788:

> *...The German Gentleman, Mr. Wilming, offered to engage a Gardener for me and to send him in a ship from Bremen. ...he is to be a compleat Kitchen Gardener with a competent knowledge of Flowers and a Green House.*

In another letter to his manager, Washington wrote:

> *...these trees to be Planted without any order or regularity, and at the South all the clever kind of Trees (especially flowering ones) that can be got.*

We are told by Egolf and Andrick in the *The Lagerstroemia Handbook-Checklist* that Washington received **Lagerstroemia indica** and **Lagerstroemia reginae** seed from the East Indies. These were delivered in 1799 on the ship *George Barclay*. A 1982 book, *The Gardens & Grounds at Mount Vernon* written by Elizabeth Kellam de Forest confirms that one of Washington's "clever trees" was crapemyrtle. One other source, Robert B. Fisher's *A List of Ornamental Trees and Shrubs Noted in the Writings of George Washington*, further adds support to this statement. Fisher served as horticulturist at Mount Vernon from 1945 to 1979.

Then we find that in 1917 all crapemyrtle were removed from the grounds of Mount Vernon by Charles S. Sargent because he could not prove they had grown there during Washington's time. He was the director of the Arnold Arboretum, and was serving in a consulting capacity for the Mount Vernon Association which operated the grounds.

According to Dr. Ernst Stuhlinger, Jeffersonian scholar and NASA rocket scientist, very well-kept records of Thomas Jefferson's Monticello gardens prove that he did not grow **Lagerstroemia**.

The Southern Nurseries of Washington, near Natchez in Adams County, Mississippi, published a very complete catalog for the years of 1853 and 1854. The owner, Thomas Affleck, was a prolific writer and fine plantsman. His extensive plant list, which included many fruiting and flowering plants, said of our subject,

> *The Crape Myrtle is one of our most beautiful ornamental Shrubs, through here forming trees from 20 to 25 feet high, or more in favorable localities. Nothing can be more showy; and it continues so many months in bloom. We have only the pink variety, until recently, when we procured two others—one a lilac-purple, and the other a bright rosy purple, both most beautiful. Except in color, they closely resemble the old sort.*

An 1872 edition of a "descriptive catalog" from M. Cole & Co.'s Atlanta Nurseries, of Atlanta, Georgia, lists two crapemyrtle: **Lagerstroemia vulgaris**, Purple Flowering Crapemyrtle, and **Lagerstroemia rosea**, Pink Flowering Crapemyrtle.

Hoskins Shadow, the famous Winchester, Tennessee nurseryman, relates that during his employment in 1926 at Griffing Nurseries of Beaumont, Texas, most crapemyrtle were grown from seed. The discovery in their field of two special seedlings led to asexual propagation of crapemyrtle and added promotion of the plant. Their catalog for those years listed **Lagerstroemia indica corrulea nana**, Dwarf Blue Crapemyrtle, **Lagerstroemia indica lilac nana**, Lilac Crapemyrtle, and **Lagerstroemia indica alba**, White Weeping Crapemyrtle.

5

Crapemyrtles make big blotches of color out of the hot sunshine.

Recent Crapemyrtle Advances

This late afternoon photo is the original Lagerstroemia fauriei as it was found on a Japanese island in 1956. (photo credit to Dr. John Creech, Hendersonville, North Carolina)

Yakushima has been called a "plant collector's paradise."

The history of crapemyrtle development in the U.S. was slow and simple, limited only to selections of volunteer seedlings by nurserymen and gardeners. This deliberate development got a great boost of energy with the appearance of Dr. Donald Egolf.

To improve the historic natural attractiveness and desirability of crapemyrtle, Dr. Egolf, a research horticulturist at the United States National Arboretum in Washington, DC, focused on **Lagerstroemia indica** breeding and selection in an effort to eliminate problems of powdery mildew.

Six cultivars were chosen, named, and introduced: Catawba, Conestoga, Potomac, and Powhatan in 1967; Seminole and Cherokee in 1970. Although these were notable improvements, Dr. Egolf realized that he could not reach his goal with *intraspecific* hybridization (crossing two plants of one species) of **Lagerstroemia indica**.

The inquisitive mind of scientist Dr. John L. Creech, of the New Crops Research Branch, United States Department of Agriculture, led to the next and most exciting chapter of this **Lagerstroemia** adventure.

Creech was aware of the nineteenth-century writings of a Japanese botanist listing **Lagerstroemia fauriei** among a census of all the plants on a steep, fourteen-mile-wide, volcanic-mountain island called Yakushima.

Yakushima is very remote and lies at the edge of the China Sea at the southern-most tip of Japan. For those who think of crapemyrtle as a plant of the old South, it is most revealing to learn about the environment of its origin.

Dr. Creech reported that the Yakushima island had long been a collecting ground for Japanese botanists. It has been called a "plant collector's paradise." Eleven-hundred species of plants are listed for this island. The vegetative ranges include a coastal savanna of mangroves near the sea, broad-leaved evergreen forests up to 1,800 feet, and above that a

While rock-hopping on a mountain river, about 1300 feet above the sea, late in the afternoon dusk, they saw the golden foliage of their quarry.

vast stand of conifers, mainly **Cryptomeria** and fir, with some deciduous trees. Above 5,500 feet, a sub-alpine climate prevails in which most plants are dwarfed.

Creech described the mysterious island as "King Kong-like" and even today, forty years later, the island has only a few small settlements, a bit of tourist activity and logging of **Cryptomeria**. The **Cryptomeria** is especially prized for the beautiful wood grain which is used as veneer for Japanese homes.

Lagerstroemia fauriei had never been in cultivation and only appeared in the literature. Creech knew of the 1914 visit to that island of Dr. E. H. Wilson, an Arnold Arboretum plant hunter, in which Wilson evidently overlooked **Lagerstroemia fauriei**. Wilson was a renowned plant detective, and because of his many travels, was called "Chinese Wilson" by some co-workers.

Hoping to locate the plant to at least preserve the germplasm, Creech made a trip to the Japanese island in 1956.

Creech and a friend, a Japanese botanist, were put into a small boat from a ship, then rowed to Yakushima to begin searching for the special **Lagerstroemia** as well as other plants of interest. For three to four weeks, they had no success. Then while rock-hopping on a mountain river, about 1300 feet above the sea, late in the afternoon dusk, they saw the golden foliage of their quarry.

Although the two botanists thoroughly examined the area, only the one mature specimen, near thirty feet tall, was found. Because of the great amount of viable seed produced by the **Lagerstroemia fauriei** in the American South, it would seem that other seedlings might have existed in the area or at the foot of the mountain and mouth of the river. None, however, were to be found.

Creech reported, "It was evident that it would soon be extinct in the wild." This work was done in

Donald Egolf in the greenhouse.

the autumn, so seed were collected and returned to the Plant Introduction Station in Glenn Dale, Maryland.

The seed were germinated and resulting seedlings were distributed to a long list of nurseries and gardens all across the U.S. for evaluation. All of the selections now in the trade and parents of the hybrids came from these seed. So all hybrids now in cultivation have this single plant in their ancestry. Creech and Dr. Sylvester G. "Skip" March, a National Arboretum horticulturist, made a second trip to the mountain island in 1976. They discovered more plants, and seed were again returned. Later trips have returned even more seed.

At the time of this first introduction, no one was aware that **Lagerstroemia fauriei** was strongly resistant, and perhaps even immune, to powdery mildew, a quality **Lagerstroemia indica** lacks. No one knew that in this tall and wide-growing species was the promise for the next generation of beauty in the crapemyrtle world.

Lagerstroemia fauriei provides an arching, vase-shaped form; larger, light-green leaves; small, white flowers; and a rapid growth rate. The outstanding attribute of this species is its great resistance to powdery mildew. Another significant characteristic of this crapemyrtle is its showy trunk surface, with the exfoliation of the outer layer exposing a superb silky-smooth, cinnamon-to-burgundy interior bark.

Dr. Egolf believed that mildew resistance could be increased by *interspecific* hybridization (that is, crossing two species) of **Lagerstroemia indica** and **Lagerstroemia fauriei**. His previous efforts had involved only varieties of **Lagerstroemia indica**. This belief proved to be true, and therein lies the beginning of the new and wonderful cultivars from the Arboretum work, which was financed by our Department of Agriculture.

Of these new selections, an ardent crapemyrtle enthusiast and garden writer, William Lanier Hunt, of

Lagerstroemia fauriei

Chapel Hill, North Carolina, wrote in the *Raleigh News and Observer*:

> *…the old purple crapemyrtles have been married up to some of their Asiatic cousins, to produce new varieties in all the colors and shades of the rainbow, and in all sizes, from dwarf to big trees. Crapemyrtles make big blotches of color out of the hot sunshine.*

Through the years, plant enthusiasts have savored the beauty of **Lagerstroemia indica**. One of those, Dr. Clarence Poe, editor of *Progressive Farmer* magazine for 67 years, once wrote about crapemyrtle:

> *How can we make the South "A Land of Beauty?" By having crepe myrtles at every home. For no other plant furnishes -1) so much beauty -2) for so long a time -3) with so little trouble. Called by the Japanese "The Flower of 101 days," mine start blooming June 15 and really keep on for 100 days.*

At his death in 1964, readers of his magazine planted more than one hundred thousand crapemyrtle to honor his memory.

Crapemyrtle In American Cities

In 1965, I attended a Southern Nurserymen's Association meeting in Norfolk, Virginia when Fred Heutte, that city's superintendent of parks, promised to make the city a "crapemyrtle capital." He accomplished his goal by placing over forty-thousand plants which today are magic summer showpieces. In Decatur, Alabama, Dr. Frank Philpot and Mrs. Gertrude Truss labored for years, influencing citizens of that North Alabama town to plant about sixty-thousand **Lagerstroemia** and in Shelbyville, Tennessee civic leaders also sponsored its use for citywide plantings. Throughout the South, many have chosen crapemyrtle for their beautification efforts. The results will be valued for generations.

In Chapel Hill, North Carolina, an all-volunteer group sponsors a yearly, week-long Crape Myrtle Festival. The funds generated go to local HIV/AIDS service and education agencies. Crapemyrtle can serve many purposes.

Caddo Crapemyrtle

9

Crapemyrtle Names

10

The *Lagerstroemia Handbook/Checklist* lists other regional names for **Lagerstroemia indica** as "Flower of the South," "Gastragna," "Gastragnier," "Lagastragna," "Lagastragnier," "Lagerrose," "Lilac of India," and "Lilac of the South." The Japanese name is "Saru Suberi."

Spelling of the word "crapemyrtle" disturbs some and leads often to the use of "crepemyrtle" or "crape myrtle," and sometimes "crape-myrtle."

My friends, including Eddie Anderson, a Virginia retail nurseryman par excellence, and Dr. John Floyd, editor of *Southern Living* magazine, have discussed this spelling with me at length. Both insist upon using crepemyrtle. Floyd says, "The plant is too nice to be a 'crap'-myrtle." David Chopin, a developer of several miniature crapemyrtle, prefers the spelling crepe-, because of the similarity of the ruffled flower petal and crepe paper. And I must admit I have a note where my father wrote the word, using the spelling and the space, crepe myrtle.

Most authorities, including the last edition of *Standardized Plant Names,* Dr. Michael Dirr's *Manual of Woody Landscape Plants*, and Dr. Carl Whitcomb's *Know It and Grow It* spell the name as I have here. However, *Hortis III* by the Baileys and Dr. Harrison Flint's *Landscape Plants for Eastern North America* both use 'crape myrtle.' Either spelling is generally accepted but now would be the perfect time for all to agree to use the spelling crapemyrtle. The commonly used nickname "crape" is totally unsuitable for these outstanding members of the plant world.

It is interesting that the plant species was named "indica" rather than "chinensis," since it is indigenous to China, and not India.

The products of the breeding and selection program at the National Arboretum, especially those managed by Dr. Egolf, all have names of American Indian tribes. He chose these because he wanted his work to be known by a distinctively American symbol. There were plenty of names from which to choose that had never been used for plants. His assistant, Ruth Dix, remembers that Dr. Egolf would try names out with the staff before making his final selection. It was important to him that the name fit the cultivar.

In Australia, Fleming's Nurseries of Monbulk, Victoria, introduced several of the selections from the National Arboretum group to their country in 1995. The campaign resulted in great success and acceptance of crapemyrtle as a major flowering tree for the first time. They marketed them as "Indian Summer Crepe Myrtle, the Dream Tree, for year-round perfection."

A note about naming the Carl Whitcomb cultivars might be instructive. He chose the name, as an example, **Lagerstroemia indica** Whit II with "Whit II" being the cultivar name. Each of these cultivars is also given a trademark name, in this case, Dynamite. As long as Whitcomb meets certain legal requirements, this name, when registered with the Patent and Trademark office, is exclusively his and cannot be used for any other plant. The patent expires, but the trademark goes on forever. Roses and other plants have been marketed for years using trademarks to indicate origin or guarantee quality and to increase sales.

Eddie Anderson, mentioned above, has used his enthusiasm for crapemyrtle to bring great attention to his fine garden centers near Hampton, Virginia. His "Crepemyrtle Festival" included promotions with the newest cultivars, special store decorations, watercolor paintings of crapemyrtle, and even "Crepemyrtle Dollars." Garden centers across the South have jumped on this bandwagon, finding crapemyrtle can bring in the summer traffic.

Dr. Donald R. Egolf

Our story of crapemyrtle development would be very short were it not for Dr. Donald R. Egolf. His vision of the plant's possibilities, ability to put the elements together, and commitment to carry out his vision, are the reasons we have our wonderful new cultivars.

Egolf was born into a farming family in Osterburg, Pennsylvania on August 27, 1928. As a boy he won numerous awards raising calves and chickens. He received degrees from Pennsylvania State University and Cornell University, focusing on plant breeding, cytology and floriculture. He did research on **Viburnum** in England while on a Fulbright scholarship.

His first and last job began in 1958 as a research horticulturist for the United States Department of Agriculture, at the National Arboretum in Washington, DC. Egolf there began a life-long study of breeding and evaluation of **Abelia**, **Cercis**, **Coreopsis**, **Hamamelis**, **Hibiscus**, **Lagerstroemia**, **Malus**, **Prunus**, **Pyracantha**, **Styrax**, **Syringa**, and **Viburnum**.

Among the many honors he received were the American Association of Nurserymen's Norman J. Coleman Award, the Silver Seal Award of the National Council of Garden Clubs, and the Chicago Horticultural Society's Hutchinson Award for Professional and Scientific Accomplishment, Significant in Furthering Horticultural Progress. Egolf held many memberships in professional societies. Among them were the American Association of Botanic Gardens and Arboreta, the American Genetics Association, the American Hibiscus Society, the American Horticultural Society, the American Society for Horticultural Science, the International Lily Society, and the Royal Horticultural Society.

The National Arboretum is the international registration authority for cultivars of **Lagerstroemia**, **Pyracantha**, and **Viburnum**. Dr. Egolf managed these programs and served as registrar. He developed descriptive checklists for both **Lagerstroemia** and **Pyracantha**, with a

11

Donald Egolf and the author appreciate the world's first large Natchez in Washington.

The heart of his work was improved resistance to insects and diseases; more beautiful flowers, leaves, and form; and increased winter hardiness.

Viburnum checklist pending, all to better serve the horticultural world's organized knowledge.

The heart of his work, in all genera, was improved resistance to insects and diseases; more beautiful flowers, leaves, and form; and increased winter hardiness.

Egolf designed a cooperative system of nurseries and gardens for evaluation of his best plants. Even today, these nurseries continue to provide information and adequate numbers of the cultivars for distribution after introduction.

Introductions of his breeding results began in 1966 with **Hibiscus rosa-sinensis** (Vulcan) and four **Lagerstroemia indica**: Catawba, Conestoga, Potomac, and Powhatan. Dr. Egolf introduced five **Hibiscus**, two **Malus**, six **Pyracantha**, eighteen **Viburnum**, and a total of twenty-six **Lagerstroemia**. Many potentially outstanding plants from his work remain in the evaluation stage and a number will become a part of our gardening future. Egolf died at age 62 on December 7, 1990, as a result of injuries received in an automobile accident.

The story of his life's work may best be told in the comments of those who worked with him: Ruth Dix, a National Arboretum research horticulturist, said, "Dr. Egolf was a brilliant man. His was a rare talent that superbly combined the elements of horticulturist, plantsman, plant geneticist, and scientist. It was an honor and a privilege to work for someone of his caliber. His personal and professional modesty, his willingness to share information, and to teach and guide others was an inspiration to me."

Don Shadow, a Tennessee nurseryman, also remembered Egolf's dedication to excellence. "His criteria were very rigorous," Shadow said. "He often said he did not want to name an inferior plant. Others do breeding work, but they never seem to turn out the material like he did. He had the ability to select plants that had potential and to work with growers to get them into production."

The serene beauty of crapemyrtle is apparent even in snow.

"The person I saw was totally dedicated and totally connected to other professionals, amateurs, and the nursery industry," said Dr. Marc Cathey, who served a term as director of the National Arboretum. "He was listening to what he heard but not completely directed by it; really, he ended up leading in terms of developing exceptional shrubs." Anne Andrick Stamper, who worked as Egolf's assistant for more than twenty years, probably knew him best.

"He was a strict taskmaster, a perfectionist, brilliant, capable, generous, loyal, rather prim; a very private person who presented a tough exterior but was really a marshmallow," Stamper said. "And he was not one to give up easily. If he believed something was right, he would fight for it. He was conversant in any subject you could talk about—art, carpentry, music, travel, politics, the economy, not just genetics and horticulture. And he would not approve my making these comments."

Dr. Mike Dirr, horticulture professor, writer, and researcher at the University of Georgia, summed up Egolf's legacy to the plant-breeding world.

"There isn't a person who has had a broader effect on woody plant breeding in the United States. His best days in a sense are yet to come."

He was not one to give up easily. If he believed something was right, he would fight for it.

Breeding Crapemyrtle

Dr. Donald Egolf demonstrates the use of a cloth bag to prevent insect delivery of unknown pollen to the flowers.

14

My dictionary defines "meticulous" as extremely careful and precise. As I learned more and more about Dr. Egolf's National Arboretum **Lagerstroemia** breeding techniques, that word became a guiding principle. Any tiny error would destroy their efforts.

The successful breeding process begins with setting the objective. One must decide what he is attempting to obtain. Does he want greater insect and disease resistance or improvement of flower, fruit, foliage, habit of growth, hardiness range or tolerance to environmental stress?

The stock plants which will be used must be carefully evaluated. Knowledge of every important attribute should be considered before starting the work.

Because even the smallest breeding project means dealing with large numbers of seedlings, it is absolutely essential to establish an accurate and thorough system of record-keeping.

Numbers are used rather than rewriting the name of the plants each time. A card is used for each female parent listing the male parent, date of pollination, date of seed collection, and number of seeds obtained.

Seed lots should be assigned a code number, and records must be kept showing the date of sowing and the number of seedlings obtained. Seedlings would also be assigned a code number, and regular evaluations must be made and recorded.

The breeding process actually begins with collecting the pollen. Flowers selected to supply the pollen are picked in the morning since crapemyrtle blooms open and begin to shed pollen early in the day. When picked, the flowers are placed in labeled paper bags and kept refrigerated. While holding the flower above folded waxed paper, the anthers are removed with forceps. The anthers are refrigerated in labeled gelatin capsules until they are ready for use.

Next, the plants to be used as female parents are emasculated. Working with each inflorescence, any flowers which have begun to open and shed pollen must be discarded. The petals and the anthers from each bud are carefully removed. *The pistil must not be damaged.*

If the breeder is working outdoors, paper bags must be used as covers to prevent insects from spreading unwanted pollen which would contaminate the work. This is not necessary in a lab or greenhouse.

There absolutely must be no cross-contamination. Tools must be rinsed in alcohol each time a different flower or lot of pollen is used. Hands must also be rinsed with alcohol between changes of flower or pollen.

There absolutely must be no cross-contamination.

Using a separate small brush for each batch of pollen, a bit of pollen is brushed across the stigma. The same pollen must be used for the entire inflorescence. If bagged, that cover should be carefully removed and replaced after pollinating. A label is attached, listing the female parent first, showing the cross and date of pollination. Repeat pollinations are required for several days as long as any fresh styles are remaining. Any new buds appearing in the inflorescence must be immediately removed before they can open and shed pollen.

The crapemyrtle should be checked regularly for seed set. As the seed pods ripen, they must be removed, labeled and stored until time for cleaning and sowing.

The evaluation and testing of the seedlings as they grow and flower may take several years. This again requires careful documentation. It is entirely possible that hundreds of thousands of plants may follow this procedure for a single new cultivar.

Each hybrid's pedigree is listed in the cultivar discussion sections. To demonstrate the complexity of some of this breeding work, look at the ancestry of the new dwarf hybrid, Chickasaw.
{[**Lagerstroemia indica** dwarf lavender x ((**Lagerstroemia indica** dwarf red x **Lagerstroemia fauriei**) x (**Lagerstroemia indica** dwarf red x **Lagerstroemia fauriei**))] x [(**Lagerstroemia indica** dwarf red x **Lagerstroemia fauriei**) x (**Lagerstroemia indica** (Low Flame) x **Lagerstroemia fauriei**]} x {[**Lagerstroemia indica** dwarf medium pink x ((**Lagerstroemia indica** dwarf red x **Lagerstroemia fauriei**) x (**Lagerstroemia indica** dwarf red x **Lagerstroemia fauriei**))] x [(**Lagerstroemia indica** dwarf red x **Lagerstroemia fauriei**) x (**Lagerstroemia indica** (Low Flame) x **Lagerstroemia fauriei**)]}.

Dr. Margaret Pooler, of the National Arboretum, helped me understand the complexity and—how else can I say it—the meticulous nature of such breeding projects.

In 1967 **Lagerstroemia indica** dwarf red was crossed with **Lagerstroemia fauriei** resulting in three seedlings, which were called 5489, 5493, and 5548. Also in 1967, **Lagerstroemia indica** (Low Flame) was crossed with **Lagerstroemia fauriei**, giving us seedling 5498.

In 1972, 5493 was crossed with 5548 giving us seedling 7258, and 5489 was crossed with 5498 resulting in seedling 8745.

Time was allowed for careful evaluation of the many seedlings grown from each of these crosses and those used for the next work were judged to be superior to the many which were destroyed.

In 1979, **Lagerstroemia indica** dwarf lavender was crossed with 7258, resulting in 8749 and **Lagerstroemia indica** medium pink was also crossed with 7258, giving us 8748.

Then in 1986, 8749 met 8745 giving 8972 and 8748 also was crossed with 8745 resulting in 8973. After careful watching and evaluation, in 1989, these two, 8972 and 8973 were bred and gave us Chickasaw.

So, Chickasaw is actually 37.5 percent **Lagerstroemia fauriei**, 25 percent **Lagerstroemia indica** dwarf red, and 12.5 percent of each of the following three **Lagerstroemia indica**: Low Flame, dwarf lavender, and dwarf medium pink.

All breeding must start with individual plants. Dr. Egolf began his program with those received from several nurserymen and researchers. Egolf's **Lagerstroemia indica** dwarf red came from Otto Spring of Okmulgee, Oklahoma, while Dr. Sam McFadden, University of Florida in Gainesville provided **Lagerstroemia indica** dwarf lavender and **Lagerstroemia indica** dwarf medium pink.

A meticulous process? Indeed. But what glorious, ever-lasting results!

Crapemyrtle Propagation

Undercutting crapemyrtle liners.

"Easy" and "rewarding" are adjectives that fittingly describe crapemyrtle. Easy is surely the word to describe crapemyrtle propagation.

"Easy" and "rewarding" are adjectives that fittingly describe crapemyrtle. Easy is surely the word to describe crapemyrtle propagation. Using either softwood or hardwood cuttings, root cuttings, division, or seed, the propagation process seldom fails. Propagators find a more difficult problem in the essential separating of varieties, and in achieving absolute certainty that no mix-up among these cultivars is allowed. Accurately identifying and separating dormant plants, especially young liners, is almost impossible.

In the years before Harvey Templeton of Winchester, Tennessee outlined his softwood production technique, the preferred system for increasing crapemyrtle, and most other deciduous flowering shrubs, was dormant hardwood cuttings.
In the 1950s, Templeton developed his productive ideas of interrupted mist techniques, employing an electronic leaf controller, which greatly simplified high-humidity softwood propagation.

The hardwood process begins with dormant summer-growth sticks, three to six feet long, being cut as quickly after defoliation as possible, from well-cared-for stock blocks. These sticks are then stored, buried in sawdust or shingletow, to protect them from desiccation and frost.

In March, eight-inch cuttings are sawed from these sticks and in April, they are stuck seven inches deep, two inches apart, in field rows. With proper irrigation, these cuttings should root and grow, depending upon the variety, 12 to 24 inches by fall. Rooting percentages vary according to the quality of the stored wood and the environmental conditions of the summer. Stands varying from 30 to 80 percent are normal. This procedure is less expensive, but the results vary greatly, and only occasionally are excellent. The harvest process begins with digging and heavy pulling. Grading, counting, and bunching are required to prepare these liners for shipping.

The word "liner" is used in the nursery trade to describe a small rooted plant, ready for planting or "lining out." The stocky plants produced in this way give good results when properly stored and then planted.

During the winter, when the bareroot plants are stored in a warehouse, each plant must be handled several times, before being tied into shippable bunches. Always present in this work environment is a quinine-like taste that occurs in the room. The roots, when handled, give an overpowering flavor to the air and subsequently to the workers' mouths. Elsewhere this book makes mention of the medical value of crapemyrtle; this palpable airborne manifestation might be evidence of that possibility.

Divisions (pieces of root and stem) and root cuttings (pieces of the root) are similar ways to propagate a crapemyrtle. Neither method is efficient

Very nice liners are produced in 4.5 inch pots (about a quart) in one summer with softwood propagation.

17

The word "liner" is used in the nursery trade to describe a small rooted plant, ready for planting or "lining out."

This simple adaptation of the hardwood cutting process will work for any home gardener.

18

Strong and well rooted liners are harvested from hardwood cuttings.

in today's world of nursery production. In either case, dormant parts of a plant are prepared and planted in a way similar to the hardwood cutting process.

Softwood cuttings may be taken from actively growing stems any time in the period they are available. When these are stuck in sand, peat, pine bark, or any combination of usual rooting media, and under mist, near-perfect stands are the norm.

These cuttings may be "direct-stuck" into pots or tubes, eliminating the job of potting from a rooting bed. A few cultivars, including Caddo and Wichita, for example, root well only when the earliest available wood is used under mist, and often a **Lagerstroemia fauriei** such as Kiowa will be contrary and not root at all.

Growth regulators such as indolebutyric acid (termed IBA in the trade) will speed root initiation, but are often unnecessary since perfect rooting is common in two to three weeks, with 120°F daytime temperature and 100 percent humidity in ventilated beds.

This most common method of propagation is fine except for one worry: how to slow the growth of these fast-moving plants before the fall frosts can freeze and kill them. The use of plastic as greenhouse covers or as "microfoam" blankets for protection is a method often used in the industry to save these plants. These plastic products act as a snow-like blanket covering the over-wintering crapemyrtle.

Seed are an unacceptable way for nurserymen to increase **Lagerstroemia**. Although easy to germinate, seed lead to mongrelization of the population. We have fought that annoyance with our careful selection routines. A plant geneticist can control the breeding process, selecting each parent for desirable attributes, in which seed are the necessary element. Otherwise, seed production just causes trouble. Often in stock rows, volunteer seedlings are a major concern. Control of these by cultivation or pre-emergent herbicides is essential.

There is, however, an easy and inexpensive way to root-your-own for home gardeners, who wish to share the perfect crapemyrtle with a friend. It is an

Regular misting maintains 100% humidity in the greenhouse all day long. Temperatures can range up to 120°F.

adaptation of the hardwood cutting method already described.

Several pencil-sized cuttings should be made from the selected plant after frost, but before hard freezes come. Three to five cuttings may be stuck in a used nursery container, at least as large as a one-gallon can, preferably larger. One inch of the top of the cutting should remain above the soil which should be an organic, well-drained, garden soil. Be *especially* sure that the soil is well-drained.

The schedule in north Alabama would be:

- Early November: fill containers, take and stick cuttings.
- Through the winter: hold in cold area, but avoid hard freezes; little water or light is needed. A garage might serve well.
- Late March: move to a sunny spot in garden, keep watered. During extremely cold weather cover with a ventilated, translucent milk jug.
- After 6 to 12 inches of new growth the crapemyrtle may be planted. Remember that full sun is essential.

This program can be adapted to any climate where **Lagerstroemia** are found. It is almost foolproof, though it is not perfect. That is why we stick more than one cutting in each container.

And, perhaps best of all, no license is required.

This program can be adapted to any climate where Lagerstroemia are found.

Stacked bunches of hardwood cuttings are ready to be planted.

Transplanting & Culture

Larger crapemyrtle can be easily moved in all seasons using earth rootballs.

I have planted crapemyrtle in every month of the year, and no great problems have occurred.

Even the greenest gardener can have great success when planting crapemyrtle. Whether the plant is bareroot, from a pot or container, or in an earth-ball, when one uses proper horticultural practices near-perfect results are to be expected. Crapemyrtle's requirements for soil types, water, nutrients, and season of planting are easily met in most moderate climates.

Crapemyrtle grow in most soils. I have always felt we should grow our crapemyrtle on the poorest ground in our nursery fields. If extreme pHs are avoided and sufficient drainage is available for the roots to be free of standing water, almost any soil will do. Fine specimens can be found in the pine bark and peat moss media of container nurseries, or heavy black loam, or the red clay of some southern soils.

Although **Lagerstroemia** prefer hot and dry conditions, it is very important to provide adequate water to new plantings. Once the roots of the new plant are established and have adapted to the location, little water is needed.

In the very hottest and driest summers, the effect of drought on the flowers is seen when they abort by failing to open or seem to scorch after a fine start. Similarly, the leaves will wilt and appear to lose their natural luster. In these periods, deep watering will allow for normal flowering and growth. Too much water, either from Mother Nature or from irrigation, can promote late juvenile growth that will often be damaged by an early frost.

Nurseries growing crapemyrtle must add fertilizers to achieve adequate size for the needs of their customers. Once a crapemyrtle is established in a landscape there is little need for fertilizer. In many cases, adding nutrients causes an effect similar to inappropriate watering: late, tender growth that is often frozen and killed in the fall.

Large specimens usually perform best when planted during the dormant season. This timing allows the roots to become well-established before spring growth appears, when they are called upon to begin their work of pumping water and nutrients to the growing areas of the plant. Smaller container or bareroot plants can be moved in any season, but if transplanted in hot summer, water must be provided as needed.

I have planted crapemyrtle in every month of the year, and no great problems have occurred. The common sense care that is provided to any planting is sufficient for good results.

Applying a thin blanket of mulch, leaves, bark or straw will level out the variations in temperature and moisture, further promoting success.

Some of this common sense should be used in choosing the site for planting. One of the most asked questions about crapemyrtle, "Why don't my crapemyrtle flower?" is invariably answered with another question, "Did you plant them in the shade?" It is important to remember that these lovely crapemyrtle perform best *only* in full sun! Choose a sunny location, with well-drained, natural soil and the greatest possible air circulation, and you'll have happy and beautiful crapemyrtle.

Every summer, on my way to work in Huntsville, Alabama, I observe a revealing aspect of the plant I love so well. A neighborhood Burger King restaurant was landscaped several years ago using Regal Red crapemyrtle on a border along the property line, with another group of Regal Red beside the building. Those near the reflected heat of the windows *always* come into flower two weeks before those out in the open area. The only possible cause for this is the mini-climate caused by the heat-gathering brick, glass and concrete. Crapemyrtle prefer full sun and lots of hot weather.

Often a crapemyrtle planted in the dormant season will not begin growing until very late in its first summer, causing concern for the gardener. At times we have seen this troublesome lack of activity last until August when, with great energy, shoots appear, and by fall we have a fine plant. Once a customer suggested his plants were in a coma! This sleeping phenomenon is usually a result of dehydration of the plant while in storage, and can be overcome by soaking the plant in water—both roots and top—for several hours before planting.

"Why don't my crapemyrtle flower?" "Did you plant them in the shade?"

Yuma Crapemyrtle

The fullness of a Yuma bloom.

I believe the 24-hour summertime heat is responsible for our flower shows.

From a 1939 catalog from Fraser Nurseries of Birmingham, Alabama, I found that this problem is not new:

Frequently crapemyrtle remain perfectly dormant most or all the first summer after planting, in the majority of cases starting growth the following spring. Many, however, after having life in them for months die without starting growth. We cannot be responsible for such losses.

I have visited several places in which I expected crapemyrtle would flourish, only to find no specimens of quality and few local gardeners trying to grow them. Southern England, the north island of New Zealand, and our Western states of Washington and Oregon are examples of those areas. I have explored this absence with several nurserymen, and the consensus is although these environments have good sunlight, moderate winters, and adequate moisture, they lack the *hot* weather found in the South where we see the finest displays.

It is also possible low nighttime temperatures could affect flowering, but I believe the 24-hour summertime heat is responsible for our flower shows. Doris Briggs, a noted Washington nurserywoman, points out beautiful **Lagerstroemia** plantings in Oregon's Willamette Valley, where the summer temperatures are among the highest in the Northwest. Australian nurseries are beginning to offer our National Arboretum cultivars with great success and acceptance. Earlier attempts, in the Melbourne area, to use a group of **Lagerstroemia indica** from selections made in France were less satisfactory.

Crapemyrtle can be used for many purposes. One unusual use is that made by Nicholas Dawidoff in a newspaper article describing Eudora Welty, the Southern writer. "Ms. Welty speaks in a gentle voice that is as Mississippi as crapemyrtle."

These are versatile plants.

Choosing Crapemyrtle

In a recent afternoon conversation, Nick Shields, a human-engineer psychologist who studies normal people's behavior for NASA, related to me an interesting observation. Nine times out of ten, he said, those who choose a flowering plant will first decide on the flower color. Before thinking about foliage, form, thorns, or landscape effects, flower color is why they want to buy the plant.

When working with bedding plants, roses, or most any of the common landscape plants, color *is* their most important consideration. At blooming time the plant must complement the house, the background, or other plants nearby and hopefully do what the buyer wants. A seasonal color scheme could be badly upset with a poor choice.

Crapemyrtle present a different set of options than most landscape plants. Since they grow in sizes ranging from small, compact garden shrubs to the tall, broad trees we see in the Deep South, color of bloom and habit of growth can be selected simultaneously.

Horticultural common sense dictates that a cultivar should first be chosen for its ability to withstand the winters of the planned site. Often in a landscape setting, protection provided by buildings, fences or walls, and other features may broaden these choices and allow the use of less hardy cultivars.

There are four groups of users: home gardeners, landscape architects, retail nurserymen, and wholesale growers. Each has different needs and expectations. After the hardiness decision, homeowners should evaluate the location planned for the crapemyrtle. If that space is unlimited, then the flower's color may be considered. But if the garden is crowded, a smaller, more fitting cultivar should be used. Once that step is taken, other garden elements can affect the decision, including all other colors in the planting, maintenance requirements, the desired season of maximum effectiveness, fall foliage and bark displays.

Marcus D. Byers

Nine times out of ten, those who choose a flowering plant will first decide on the flower color.

If crapemyrtle is sized properly cruel pruning can be avoided.

If the crapemyrtle is sized properly for the available space, the cruel pruning employed to squeeze a tree into an unnatural form can be avoided. Among those with the proper size and habit, there are usually several choices of bloom color.

Landscape architects and landscape contractors must answer questions in another order. Their first concern must be the clients' wishes and specifications, followed by the price and availability. Next, almost always, should be the form or habit of growth. Within the chosen range of sizes, many options are available such as color of flower and bark, time and length of effective flowering, maintenance requirements, fall foliage displays, and ease of transplanting. Our lists of crapemyrtle cultivars, provided in the appendix, will help in making the best choices.

Retail nurseries and garden centers want fast turnover. For them, bloom color and an early season flower are the most important crapemyrtle features. Other properties of crapemyrtle are secondary if the plants are well-grown and properly priced. Many of the best garden centers now offer the new cultivars and greater selections, adding more value to their product.

Wholesale nurserymen, growers who must guess years in advance what the public and landscape professionals will want, have an entirely different rank of guidelines. Their selection of which varieties to offer will usually be based on past sales records, visits with their primary customers, speed of growth, and information on new cultivars coming on the market.

Minor considerations are habit and an appealing name. Flower color is an essential part of planning the mix of crapemyrtle, because wholesale nurserymen know that the percentages rarely change. Over half the crapemyrtle sold at retail each year have red flowers. Next in popularity come pink flowers, then white, followed finally by lavender. Sales of other flowering plants follow this same pattern. Most of the gardening public choose color first.

But remember: all these thoughts are of little aid if we forget crapemyrtle do best in full sun!

Grading Crapemyrtle

The American Association of Nurserymen does a special service for the industry. A committee of the AAN, on which I have served, publishes an updated American Standard for Nursery Stock every five years. The information is put through rigorous testing and is finally approved by the American National Standards Institute, Inc. This gives a regulated procedure to describe accurately or specify plants for all types of uses.

Crapemyrtle liners are normally sold in pots or as bareroot shrubs. Both buyers and sellers use these well-established sizes and methods. Larger container-grown plants are measured by container size and sometimes by height.

Large specimen trees are different. Because all shade trees are specified by trunk caliper (diameter of the trunk at six inches above the ground until the caliper reaches four inches, then at twelve inches above the groundline), and because most crapemyrtle are planted as multi-trunk trees, an uncertainty arises: should one measure only the caliper of the largest trunk, or measure all and add the calipers together, or must *all* trunks be at least the specified size?

The answer is that multi-trunk trees of all kinds are measured officially only by height, and never by caliper. So crapemyrtle grown with one trunk can be described by trunk caliper, while the usual (multi-trunk) specimens are denoted by height. Certainly both designators may be used at the same time, assuring no misunderstanding. Often, however, unrealistic specifications are written which require the caliper to be much larger than the desired cultivar will produce at the desired height. This problem is solved with experience and discussion and will probably disappear when more gardeners learn about the wide range of size choices.

Multi-trunk trees are measured officially only by height, and never by caliper.

Winter Hardiness

Crapemyrtle tolerate cold differently. A 30° morning on April 15 killed the new spring growth on Choctaw and did not affect that of Natchez.

More questions arise about the winter hardiness of crapemyrtle than about any other facet of the plant. For years, tourists from the North wanted to take this beautiful "lilac of the South" to their homes in less temperate climates. Growers and retailers saw the enormous marketing possibilities that could come from supplying a more hardy crapemyrtle to the North. A major goal of Dr. Egolf's work was to increase the range of winter limits for crapemyrtle habitat.

A number of studies have been done in the last ten years to determine the exact nature of "winter hardiness." I have worked with the Chicago Botanical Garden, the University of Georgia, the National Arboretum in Washington, other researchers, and several nurserymen in an attempt to define "winter hardiness."

We have supplied plants of all available varieties to many groups who were attempting to quantify hardiness. In general, these studies have produced inconclusive results. The data from one season's work cannot be duplicated the next year. The results from a study in Mississippi, for example, directly contradict studies from Georgia and Washington.

A quick example of these frustrating findings is taken from a report found on the internet, posted by Ellen Silva of Virginia Tech. During January and March, four-inch cuttings were taken from new wood and exposed to gradually colder temperatures. Of the lot, various cuttings were removed at 20, 15, 10, and 5 degrees Fahrenheit. These cuttings were then placed in moist sand to evaluate viability. Silva reports, "Results were variable, making it impossible to precisely rank the cultivars for hardiness."

Dr. Randy Johnson, U.S. National Arboretum geneticist, wrote in a 1993 letter:

> *In cooperation with Drs. Lindstrom and Dirr at the University of Georgia and David Byers of Byers Nursery, we investigated laboratory cold hardiness of* **Lagerstroemia** *taxa. December results showed considerable variation among the taxa, but a warm spell in January de-acclimated everything to about the same level. Correlation of our results with other studies showed very little consistency with regard to the rank of cultivars. Preliminary results suggest that the relative cold hardiness for crapemyrtle taxa is more dependent on the weather conditions and cultural practices than on the particular cultivar.*

(A note about the word "taxa" is in order. This relatively new term is the plural of "taxon." These words are used to cover all—or one—of the plants making up a taxonomic group. None of the previously available words covers the entirety of the plants making up a Genus. Species indicates a sub-genus; varieties are sub-species; cultivars, a selection of a variety, must be in cultivation; and then some plants are trademarked and registered; these word choices lack the ability to cover the entire list. Now we have taxa.)

A thoughtful look at the hardiness question may provide the answer. Weather is the prime factor. It is unpredictable and cannot be programmed. A cultivar of **Lagerstroemia** will likely act exactly the same each winter if the circumstances of its environment are exactly the same. In this real world, the weather varies greatly from year to year. That's why with crapemyrtle, as with most plants, complete reliance on the hardiness zone maps leads one to mistaken conclusions.

With crapemyrtle, there are three kinds of winter threat. Ideally, plants first receive a few gentle frosts then, as the length of daylight shortens, progressively colder weather occurs. This ends in full winter dormancy. Actually, this progression seldom happens.

Some plants go dormant normally and, even at their maximum dormancy, still cannot tolerate a hard freeze in January.

The downward march of temperatures is often interrupted by a few warm days; the carefully gathered dormancy is lost and the pattern must begin again, possibly at a lower beginning level.

First, early-fall freezes affect cultivars which go dormant later or more slowly. The Miami variety, for example, frequently suffers this type of early freeze damage.

The second threat is the extreme cold of mid-winter. Some plants go dormant normally and, even at their maximum dormancy, still cannot tolerate a hard freeze in January. Several old purple varieties were dropped from production for this reason. This winter damage caused by the season's maximum cold is the hardiness level evaluated by most researchers, and those who limit their attention to this area miss significant problems elsewhere.

The third cold weather threat to crapemyrtle is that occurring in the early spring. Some varieties, Potomac being the best example, begin growing with great vigor at the first warm weather. Mother Nature then sends a late, hard freeze resulting in major injury. I have heard complaints that crapemyrtle begins growing too early. The trouble is that the enormous stored-up energy produces new growth and destruction is inevitable. We've had large blocks of Potomac, six to eight feet tall, with no damage all winter long, killed to the ground by one of these late freezes.

My rules for maximizing winter hardiness of these beautiful plants are:

1- Choose cultivars that experience has shown to be most hardy.
2- Plant them only in full sun.
3- Never fertilize crapemyrtle.
4- Never water crapemyrtle.
5- Never prune crapemyrtle.

I realize these are extreme rules that few would choose to follow completely, but experience proves them to be reliable. The ignored, unloved, and forgotten crapemyrtle, treated with benign neglect, are those that go on year after year. In the real world, we should avoid those things that would encourage late growth, including fertilizing during the blooming period, fall watering or severe pruning. Any procedure which promotes continued growth in late fall is the enemy when we are battling to extend our northern range.

Never, of course, is a long time, so we must moderate the firm statements of my rules. The growth of a crapemyrtle is controlled by its genetic makeup and the availability of light, nutrients, suitable temperature, and water. Fertilizer applied in the fall or winter will encourage spring growth but will not cause damage the following autumn. We think our best period for adding nutrients to specimen crapemyrtle is in late autumn, just as the leaves fall. This is late enough that no growth is forced, but the roots are still active and the nutrients can be taken up into the plant. Fertilizer containing nitrogen should not, in any case, be applied between midsummer and frost. Finally, if a plant is in full sun, and fails to perform as expected, then fertilizing and pruning may be necessary for rejuvenation.

"Water is sometimes a herbicide to **Lagerstroemia**," the late Dr. J. C. Raulston, plantsman supreme, of North Carolina State University, once said.

The best **Lagerstroemia** flower shows are in the drier years. There are two occasions when plants must be watered: in times of severe drought and just after planting. But always remember, excessive fall watering will predispose the plant to damage from an early freeze.

There are ways to evaluate the depth of freeze damage when it does occur. We have found three distinct events to observe. Within a few days after the cold event, the cambium layer (the active growth area just beneath the bark) will darken. A bit of this discoloration is not especially bad, but a dark cambium is an

29

The growth of a crapemyrtle is controlled by its genetic makeup and the availability of light, heat, nutrients, and water.

30

All the work and concern about winter hardiness goes out the window if you are considering crapemyrtle in Florida.

early and sure sign of trouble. A few weeks after the drastic weather, the bark will split and large vertical gaps will appear. In the worst cases, the bark will release and can be grasped and then turned on the trunk. This is a sign of real disaster. Third, several weeks or months after the event, you can observe stem death as a result of freezing. The upright limbs near the top turn in to the center axis in a "praying-hands" manner. When this is present, plans for heavy pruning should be made.

All the work and concern about winter hardiness goes out the window if you are considering crapemyrtle in Florida. There the primary questions are: how can we extend the flowering period, eliminate aphids and powdery mildew, and avoid suckering? Norm Easey, a city horticulturist from Sarasota, told me of complaints reporting dead plants in the street medians. Inspection revealed only dormant and defoliated crapemyrtle. Do you suppose it is possible to make them bloom for twelve months?

These adaptable **Lagerstroemia** are amazing plants.

Pruning Crapemyrtle

Disagreement is always in the air when discussing crapemyrtle pruning. Dr. Ted Bilderback of North Carolina State University writes, "If we can't agree on how to spell crapemyrtle, it is not surprising that there is controversy on how to prune it."

We know that pruning encourages new growth and increases juvenility. The fact that these plants flower on new wood is sometimes an excuse for using the shears. But any heavy pruning during the summer lessens the chances for survival if winter is a threat.

There are a few reasons to prune crapemyrtle. Legitimate excuses would probably include correcting winter damage, removing suckers, and pruning for shape in winter. If the landscape architect, contractor, or home gardener carefully chooses the proper variety to match the space and other requirements, little pruning will ever be necessary. It is primarily that responsibility of choice that spurred me to put my thoughts in writing here.

Different cultivars are available now, with varying flower colors and habits of growth, to fit any situation. This should eliminate the need for pruning for form, of which we have seen far too much in the past.

Jeff Farmer and Paul Bertrand, horticulturists at Walt Disney World in Orlando, Florida, supervise pruning thousands of large crapemyrtle each year. A summer walk through the properties will convince one that they know what they are doing. Farmer and Bertrand presented a talk at the 1993 Menninger Flowering Tree Conference explaining their methods.

They teach that pruning should accentuate the natural character of the plant. In their system, lower limbs, rubbing or crossing branches, and bad crotches are first removed. Fine pruning includes taking out small twigs, dead wood and old seed heads. An open, clean wood structure encourages good air circulation and reduces powdery mildew problems.

Finally, some light pruning is done to the sides of the top to achieve a natural shape and allow the

Help! Crapemurder! Pruning like this causes pain to crapemyrtle and to crapemyrtle lovers.

Pruning should accentuate the natural character of the plant.

These unsightly "knuckles" come from bad pruning practices and result in new growth with long-lasting structural problems.

blooms to fold over individually. Unwanted sprouting and basal suckering are avoided by correctly cutting immediately above the branch collar. Sprout removal is an every-year job if not eliminated by careful and clean cuts.

A popular form is the single-cane tree or, as it is called in the trade, the "standard." For fast growing varieties, this is an appropriate habit for use on narrow planting areas such as street medians. Be certain to note, however, that when a very hard freeze comes, killing the plant to the ground, the plant must be grown all over again with extra pruning necessary to remove the unwanted stems that come from the cutting-back.

Recently, all across the South, a new phenomenon has appeared. Chazz Cox, a Florida nurseryman, termed this stump-pruning act "Crapemurdering." Some pruners head back major trunks at a convenient height below all limbs to force a large tree-type plant into a rotund form raised on fat trunks, creating a lollipop look. This procedure (done without anesthesia, I'm sure) destroys the natural beauty of a plant and unnecessarily exposes the resulting growth to breakage from ice or wind. The pencil-size stems often cannot support the weight of a full-size flower, especially when wet.

While not so noticeable in summer, with full foliage present, the winter silhouette becomes a collection of stumped canes, knuckles, and witches' brooms. The multitude of acute crotches created by this heading-back opens the door for insect egg placement and an unsightly and unnatural appearance. I place this stunt on my list of Pet Peeves!

Dr. John Floyd's March 1995 article in *Southern Living* insists that it is most important to maintain the "sculptural character" of the tree. He strongly feels that "stump-cutting" ruins any hope of the unmatched, natural beauty expected as the plant ages. And *Southern Living* in a January 1997 article suggests crapemyrtle pruning should be thought of as "training." If the proper cultivar is chosen, no pruning other than occasional thinning will be needed.

If your crapemyrtle tree has been improperly pruned or cruelly topped, it is possible to encourage future growth to develop to a more natural form. When new growth from a stubbed trunk begins, the single strongest and straightest should be left, while all others are removed. If the trunk is very large, three inches or more, the entire limb should be cut to the ground, allowing new trunks to develop properly. If the mistreatment has gone on for several seasons, leaving knots and knuckles, the disfigurement should be removed by sawing at ground level. Because crapemyrtle have so much natural vigor, you can expect recovery from the most drastic repair in about two years.

Some say removal of the maturing flower heads will force new flowering. Charlie Parkerson, a Virginia nurseryman, told me of his effort to force additional growth on the variety Regal Red after it began flowering. He cut off the flower heads before seed were formed and found that particular cultivar quickly put on new blooms, not new growth. There is a varietal difference here: some will react as Regal Red did, while others will not re-bloom as readily. With the improved, recurrent flowering of new cultivars, however, one should be satisfied with Mother Nature's planned performance, instead of attempting to manipulate flowering through pruning.

When extreme cold comes, and the woody trunks and stems are injured, these extraordinary plants can be sawed off flush with the ground. That done, a period of renewal begins. Many times, entire fields of mature plants are sawed down and a year or two later are again ready for sale. This same sawing works in home plantings and gardens. Extra, sucker-like growth is sometimes the result of this severe pruning, but selective removal will get the plant back to the three or five trunks usually desirable in tree-type crapemyrtle.

Stumpcutting crapemyrtle.

"Stump-cutting" ruins any hope of the unmatched, natural beauty expected as the plant ages.

Crapemyrtle Problems

Healthy, happy crapemyrtle are more likely to be unaffected by these insects than those under stress.

Its trouble-free nature is one of the especially nice things about crapemyrtle. Few insects prefer it over other food choices. Aphids, Japanese beetles, flea beetles, and Florida wax scale are the only important bugs that regularly affect the appearance and performance of crapemyrtle.

Healthy, happy crapemyrtle are more likely to be unaffected by these insects than those under stress. Stress can be caused by many things, such as extreme weather conditions, transplanting, misuse of pesticides, or other such changes from the norm. The four prominent crapemyrtle problems are discussed below.

Crapemyrtle Aphids

Tinocallis kajawaluokalani, also known as plant lice, are pale yellow, with the winged adults having black wings and black protuberances. They are usually found consuming the soft growing tips of the foliage and on the underside of leaves, often reducing the size, vigor, and appearance of crapemyrtle.

A second effect is, while feeding, they secrete droplets of honey dew, a sticky substance that completely covers leaves and stems and on which grows the hideous Sooty Mold fungus. Uncontrolled, this becomes a black, unsightly coating on leaves and stems. Sooty Mold does no real damage on its own, but the result is a blocking of sunlight, which slows photosynthesis and ultimately reduces vigor. The dried mold can sometimes be removed from leaves by a hard, directed water spray or the normal wear and tear of wind and rain. The mold will disappear as the plant defoliates, although remnants may continue to show on the stems for some time.

No other aphid species is found on crapemyrtle. We need no others, however, for this one can reproduce rapidly and quickly builds large populations.

Work has been done at the North Florida Research Center, near Monticello, to evaluate various cultivars' natural resistance to crapemyrtle aphid attack in landscape settings. Results of this several-year study are mixed, but they found most cultivars with high resistance to powdery mildew had the least resistance to aphids. They also found the larger-growing plants had more aphids per leaf than medium or smaller-growing plants. Crapemyrtle with some **Lagerstroemia fauriei** parentage were more likely to have an aphid problem. These aphid attacks were not related to flower color.

Informal observations by some nurserymen argue with the Florida results. Some are convinced Natchez, the very large-growing hybrid crapemyrtle, has strong resistance to aphids. Others report Tuscarora and Apalachee to be magnets for aphids.

Dr. Gary Knox, who leads the investigation at Monticello, suggests that their evaluations may have little application to crapemyrtle grown in nursery fields. A grower's experience is quite different from a landscaper's since the grower has large numbers grouped closely together and is constantly "pushing" his crop. That new growth then attracts aphids. Knox's plantings are spaced adequately for evaluation of form, a situation similar to landscapes and gardens.

Natural enemies or predators often work to hold the population of aphids in check. Some of these are lacewings, syrphid flies, ladybug beetles (both adults and larvae), praying mantids and some tiny wasps. Other work mentioned on the University of Florida internet publication summarizing "IPM Florida, Research Report BB93-4" suggests crapemyrtle may be used as attractants for these beneficials to orchards of pecans and other crops. The researchers assert the honeydew of the crapemyrtle aphid feeds twenty to thirty species of beneficial insect predators and many other bees and wasps, especially during periods of excessive drought. Large quantities of the aphids encourage these predators to stay in the area.

Sooty Mold, the aftermath of a bad aphid infestation, leaves a heavy black coating on the leaves. Control of the aphids eliminates this disaster

35

Careful attention can catch flea beetle attacks before damage occurs.

Crapemyrtle serve the greater good in many ways.

In any case, control of the aphid completely eliminates the sooty mold. Any conventional insecticide, horticultural oil, or insecticidal soap for home use will restrain crapemyrtle aphids.

Research work done at the Auburn University Experiment Station near Mobile, Alabama found the use of an Orthene slurry, painted on the trunks at the first sight of aphids, will control the problem. Information on this treatment is available from the Valent USA Corporation of Walnut Creek, California, the manufacturers of Orthene. The phone number at this writing is 800/898-2536.

The challenge is to perform timely inspections and to carefully use an insecticide when necessary. One might also release predator insects before the aphid population gets out of hand. This approach is gaining popularity as it is environmentally safe, but it is not completely dependable.

Japanese beetles

Popilla japonica are becoming Southern insects, after first being seen in New Jersey in 1916. As they came south, they found crapemyrtle to be one of their favorite taste-treats in all the plant world. Feeding on leaves, fruits and flowers, they are prominent pests for about 60 days each summer. Insecticidal control of the shiny, metallic-green and copper adults, is difficult at best. Larvae can be safely controlled with the use of milky disease spores, sprayed on the soil. Traps prepared with pheremones (sexual attractants) are now available and, when properly placed, are effective in reducing the population of adult Japanese Beetles.

Flea Beetles

Altica species, tiny, iridescent, and green-backed, appear in busloads at crapemyrtle fields. I know they must ride in buses, because there is just no natural way for them to arrive on scene as quickly as they do. These are not a big problem to homeowners or to those who have few plants. But in large growing fields these hungry bugs can cause havoc, consuming the most tender new growth. This problem is more common when plants are in a high-fertility soil. A crop can be severely impacted, slowed, or reduced to stems and roots in just a few days. Careful, regular inspection and an immediate, directed spray of mild insecticides will thwart the work of these thugs. Flea beetles have a very short life cycle, making repeated sprays essential for control.

Florida wax scale

Ceroplastes floridensis, an insect covered with a thick, protective, waxy coating, does its damage by sucking sap from the stems. Early season spraying of safe insecticides in a horticultural oil, before the coating is formed, is effective control. Later in the summer, use of a systemic insecticide which flows in the sap of the treated plant is recommended.

Borers

Once I saw an attack of borers on Natchez crapemyrtle: scattered across vigorously-growing, six-foot plants on a neighbor's farm were several injured and twisted lower limbs, evidence of the insertion of this insect's eggs. As the larva had grown and eaten its way up the stem, it had caused weakening and distortion. Entomologist Dr. Pat Cobb, of Auburn University, and Dr. Bryson James, an industry consultant, separately looked at the results and both felt this was a random attack, the aftermath of a single wandering by a passing insect, likely attracted to a crapemyrtle stressed by weather or other causes. Borers are not a concern with **Lagerstroemia**.

Flea beetles have a very short life cycle, making repeated sprays essential for control.

37

*Crapemyrtle
is a robust
and stalwart
choice for
beauty
and
timelessness.*

Powdery Mildew, crapemyrtle's worst problem, devastates the beauty of the leaves and weakens the entire plant.

Ambrosia Beetle

A Georgia Cooperative Extension Service entomologist, Dr. Beverly Sparks, recently identified a problem with Potomac crapemyrtle as being the result of an assault by **Xylosandrus crassiusculus**. She described that damage as

> ...numerous 'pin-point' sized holes along the lower trunks of the plant. Cross sections of the damaged areas revealed galleries and staining of the surrounding tissues by the introduced fungi.

Like the borer attack described above, this beetle is probably not an important pest for our future concern. Crapemyrtle apparently has attractions for all the insect world as well as plant lovers.

I should mention our good experience, at Byers Nursery Co., with a dormant (meaning it is applied during the dormant season) oil spray, combined with an insecticide and a fungicide. This seems to be a relatively safe, inexpensive, and effective control for most insect and fungus pests of plants. For the best ideas for control of your pests, you should consult experts with your extension service or other agency of your choice.

Powdery Mildew

Erysiphe lagerstroemiae, or powdery mildew, is crapemyrtle's worst problem. This fungus plague of crapemyrtle is an unsightly aggravation. It appears as a dwarfing or stunting of the leaves and flowers. Often there is a cupping and curling of the leaves before the white, powder-like mycelium is apparent. These symptoms are caused by withdrawal of nutrients and excessive respiration, according to Dr. Cynthia Westcott's *Plant Disease Handbook*.

Control of powdery mildew is tough! The mycelium can overwinter on buds. The spores are spread by wind and water. Like most fungi, it flourishes in an environment of low light and high humidity. This infection is encouraged by overhead watering and planting situations with shade and limited air movement.

Fungicides that offer some control are available, but the effectiveness ends when the product is washed off the plant. Few systemic fungicides (absorbed and circulated throughout the plant) are considered valuable although newer materials are promising improved results, especially when their use is alternated in a timely spray regimen. Altering the surrounding environment would possibly control the spread and effect, but that is not a practical solution, and practicality is a nurseryman's middle name.

Relief comes with careful selection of varieties. Through the years, more crapemyrtle have been dropped from production because of powdery mildew problems than for any other reason. Dr. Egolf's work had, as its primary goal, selection of cultivars with high resistance to this disease. Now there is sufficient information available for all to make wise choices, which can eliminate most of the mildew problems.

Leaf Spot

Cercospora lythracearum, a fungal organism, occurs on some crapemyrtle as a leaf spot. It is not a significant problem except in the deepest South where humidity is the highest.

Suckering

The small, whippy growth from latent buds at the soil line area of the plant, often called water-sprouts, is a common complaint of those who use crapemyrtle in landscape plantings. It is thought to be a problem of certain varieties but, in my experience, this is a cultural problem. Some horticulturists report suckering worse with **Lagerstroemia indica** cultivars than with the hybrids.

39

Through the years, more crapemyrtle have been dropped from production because of powdery mildew problems than for any other reason.

A bird's-eye view of Conestoga flowers reveals this cross.

When crapemyrtle is grown in a fertile and well-watered situation, the results are vigor and juvenility and possible suckering. One certain cause of this growth is improper pruning. It is very important, when removing limbs, to make the cut to leave the collar at the trunk. That done, healing is quick and complete, eliminating some risk of suckering. A soil mulch of bark, straw, or similar material may help avoid suckering.

An acquaintance, Norm Easey, is involved with the tree program in Sarasota County, Florida. There, several crapemyrtle cultivars were chosen for a major street tree planting, and suckering has caused him much concern. Costs for regular pruning and complaints from citizens have made him aware that this obstacle to satisfaction must be overcome.

Experimental work done by Dr. Gary Keever in 1988 at Auburn University has indicated an application of NAA (naphthaleneacetic acid) to the trunk will prevent this unwanted growth. This program has been successfully used on fruit and nut trees for some time. Perhaps this will be the solution to the suckering problems. Several nurseries are using a commercial product containing NAA with marked success. Called "Tre-Hold," it is labeled for use on crapemyrtle. The manufacturer, Amvac Chemical Corporation of California may be called at 714/260-1212. Dr. Keever's study shows some effect to the growth rate and ultimate size of the treated crapemyrtle.

Growers must be certain the plants they offer for sale are actually the varieties requested. Mixes are to be avoided at all costs. The remarkably viable seed of the **Lagerstroemia indica** X **fauriei** crosses increase the chance for confusion. After the heavy flowering period concludes, seed are formed and are dispersed as the seed pods open. These seed often germinate in the rows and between rows, resulting in the possibility that wood taken for the next group of cuttings might be mixed with a chance seedling of unknown quality. A well-timed program of cultivation and applications of pre-emergence herbicide, preventing normal germination, will usually eliminate this trouble. (A pre-emergent is a chemical agent, applied as a granule or liquid, which, for a period of time depending on the brand, concentration and weather, prevents the successful germination of seed in the treated area.)

All this discussion of problems must be countered with the statement that **Lagerstroemia** is one of the most disease-free and insect-free ornamentals in our palette of plants. In fact, crapemyrtle are hard to kill. Often while removing an old planting in preparation for a new field, we have regrowth for several years. Truly, crapemyrtle is a robust and stalwart choice for beauty and timelessness.

This is not a perfect world, but with crapemyrtle we do have a plant that is near perfection. No other ornamental compares to the ease of culture, beautiful performance, and rewarding resilience of this genus.

Most gardeners enjoy crapemyrtle for their beauty; others have different reasons. James A. Duke demonstrates some of those in his 1985 book, *Medicinal Plants of China:*

> *Uses: Flower: Decoction for colds. Stembark: Styptic; decoction for abscesses; cooked with pork to cure rheumatism, internal injuries, and bleeding uterus. Root: Detoxicant, diuretic, used for abdominal distention and pain, abscesses, bruises, boils, dermatitis, dysentery, edema, jaundice, Tripterygium poisoning, ulcers and vertigo. Seeds are said to contain a narcotic principle. In India the astringent roots are used as a gargle and the febrifuge bark is considered stimulant. Indochinese use the bark, flowers, and leaves as a purgative.*

41

No other ornamental compares to the ease of culture, beautiful performance, and rewarding resilience of this genus.

42

The hardest work of crapemyrtle harvesting is the pulling.

Other uses were mentioned by Egolf and Andrick. The very hard wood has been used in the construction of things requiring elasticity and strength such as ships, housing, and furniture. Different **Lagerstroemia** species have been sources for charcoal and tannin, and supplied plywood, pilings for shipping docks and power poles.

I've always known crapemyrtle is a super plant! Bo Tidwell, a Greenville, Georgia nurseryman, wrote of crapemyrtle:

> *It is tall, stately and sleek, with heavenly branches, delightful seasonal blooms, and a delicate lush foliage that whispers in the summer breeze, and rails at the advent of cold weather, with a bold array of fall colors. Even when winter has stripped her branches bare, she still stands gracefully, through all that Mother Nature can unleash, and extracts her revenge with the stark dignity of her simple form, silhouetted against the bleak winter sky, while the sheer beauty of her bark glows in the fading afternoon light.*

So, we see that crapemyrtle are fine for foliage and flower, and fine for color in both summer and winter. Some cultivar will serve in almost any sunny situation, from big to little, or even very little. The problems are few and surmountable. There is something for everyone including those with medical problems.

I've been asked, "Have you grown crapemyrtle all your life?"

I answered, "Not yet, but I intend to."

Last fall on two occasions I saw small scarlet tanagers eating crapemyrtle seeds. What fun!

Crapemyrtle, Mature Height Up to 5 feet

The first question on your test is, "What is a dwarf crapemyrtle?"

Or a dwarf holly? Or any other dwarf plant? That is a tough question and it is asked about many landscape plants, especially as those plants mature at sizes far larger than expected.

Dr. Alfred Einert addressed this with the introduction of four **Lagerstroemia indica** varieties in 1973. His work followed the developments of Otto Spring, an Okmulgee, Oklahoma nurseryman, who had for some years attempted selection of crapemyrtle with compact habits and wide ranges of flower color. Spring, who was an interesting and crusty plantsman, once wrote in a 1982 letter to *Southern Florist and Nurseryman* magazine:

> I am the foremost originator of new
> (and satisfactory) varieties and have
> been producing them since the early
> 1920s. I have produced many thou-
> sands of crosses and many outstanding
> new varieties. Most of mine are hardy
> just about all over the United States.

In 1960, Dr. Victor Watts, a vegetable breeder and head of the Department of Horticulture and Forestry at the University of Arkansas, obtained from Spring 39 different crapemyrtle. When Dr. Einert came to the program in 1970, he inherited the results of the open-field crosses done by Dr. Watts. After careful evaluation in all the varied climates in Arkansas, he introduced the four best for "annual growth rate, powdery mildew and leaf-beetle resistance, fall foliage color, and winter hardiness."

Dr. Einert introduced the four best for "annual growth rate, powdery mildew and leaf-beetle resistance, fall foliage color, and winter hardiness."

*Even
small
crapemyrtle
can get
relatively
large in
time.*

Dr. Einert wrote for the *Arkansas Farm Research* in 1967,

> *...the designation "dwarf," denotes a reduced growth rate, specifically an annual vegetative growth of 24 to 36 inches after the dormant plant has been pruned to 6 to 8 inches from the ground in early spring.*

Dr. Randy Johnson, plant breeder and Dr. Donald Egolf's successor at the United States National Arboretum in Washington, DC, spoke about this problem in a talk given to the Southern Nurserymen's Association's Research Workers' Conference of August 1993 in Atlanta. He said

> *...many of the crapemyrtle sold as "dwarfs" should be called "slow-growing," because even small crapemyrtle can get relatively large in time. Classification should be based on height at specific ages or stages of growth.*

Johnson's suggestion in part is "If the height of a crapemyrtle at age 5 years is less than 4 feet, then that plant is a 'Dwarf.'"

We have a better definition of a dwarf crapemyrtle now that the crapemyrtle breeding and selection begun by Dr. Egolf and his able assistant, Ruth Dix, is resulting in introductions. Dr. Margaret Pooler, National Arboretum scientist, has chosen Chickasaw to be distributed to botanical gardens and opened for commerce in 1997. Dwarf, midget, Lilliputian, true-to-life, small cultivars will soon be available to the trade then to the landscape contractors and the gardening world. These beauties could become a new type of bedding plant; perennial, hardy and in less need of attention and care. On trial today at several nurseries and gardens around America are the future blue ribbon winners from the National Arboretum.

Crapemyrtle, Mature Height Up to 5 feet

Victor Crapemyrtle

Ozark Spring
Crapemyrtle

Up to 5 Feet Tall

Victor Crapemyrtle

Chickasaw Crapemyrtle

Centennial Crapemyrtle

Up to 5 Feet Tall

Velma's Royal Delight Crapemyrtle

(Photo credit to Dr. John Pair, Wichita, KS)

Velma's Royal Delight Crapemyrtle

5 to 10 Feet Tall

48

Prairie Lace Crapemyrtle

Tonto Crapemyrtle

Photograph courtesy of
Fleming's Nurseries Pty. Ltd.,
Victoria, Australia.

Hopi Crapemyrtle

5 to 10 Feet Tall

5 to 10 Feet Tall

Pecos Crapemyrtle

Zuni Crapemyrtle

Photograph courtesy of
Fleming's Nurseries Pty. Ltd.,
Victoria, Australia.

Caddo Crapemyrtle

Hopi Crapemyrtle

5 to 10 Feet Tall

Acoma Crapemyrtle

Sioux & Acoma
Crapemyrtle

One word of concern: Some of these choices on trial have shown limby, run-away sports, growth with extra-long internodes. Is this to be a common occurrence on these dwarfs, or just an unhappy start on the evaluations? I'm going to believe that the selections will prove to be fine additions to our list.

I met Dr. Al Einert at a reception during a Southern Nurserymen's Association Atlanta meeting in the early 1970s. After our conversation, he shipped me each of the new **Lagerstroemia indica** seedling selections he had just introduced: Centennial, Hope, Ozark Spring, and Victor. His vision was a small, trouble-free, summer flowering plant that would be of use all across the South. Over the years two of these four selections have proven to be truly outstanding.

Centennial

This is one of the very good small crapemyrtle. Its bright purple flowers are as good as any other **Lagerstroemia**. As the summer progresses, they fade to a softer purple and last for about 70 days. The rounded, globose habit of growth requires no pruning. I've seen none that grew larger than 4 feet tall and wide. Centennial, which was named to commemorate the centennial of the University of Arkansas, celebrated in 1971, exhibits a nice reddish-yellow fall foliage color. Centennial offers good powdery mildew resistance along with acceptable winter hardiness.

Centennial offers good powdery mildew resistance along with acceptable winter hardiness.

Research Horticulturist Ruth Dix, Donald Egolf's able assistant, holds Chickasaw for all to admire.

Chicksaw

Dr. Margaret Pooler joined the staff at the U.S. National Arboretum in 1996 as leader of the plant breeding section and chose to introduce in April 1997, the first of the very dwarf **Lagerstroemia** hybrids by the American Indian name Chickasaw. We have had this cultivar on trial in Huntsville, Alabama for several years and have rated it highly in every evaluation. The pink-lavender flowers are attractive and small, and begin to bloom in mid- to late summer, later than most of its big cousins. Blooms persist till frost in most cases. Glossy dark-green leaves turn bronze-red in the fall.

The attribute which makes this one different is its size and habit. After growing in a container at the Arboretum in Washington for six years, it is a dense plant with tiny internodes, with a compact mound habit of growth. It is about twenty inches high and twenty-six inches wide. We find our specimens to be a bit smaller, but they are growing in the field and are more affected by cold and drying in that environment.

Chickasaw may not become an immediate commercial favorite because of its slow growth. The final cost of a plant ready for landscape use may be much more than other similar size choices because this dwarf will take more time to finish. Also the small stock plants produce little wood for cuttings. We find it roots readily from softwood or hardwood cuttings. This leisurely finishing may even make tissue culture impractical.

I can imagine landscape beds in downtown parks massed with this fine textured crapemyrtle flower-show performing like an azalea in bloom for the last 70 or 80 days of summer. It will be outstanding in small foundation plantings, or in rock gardens, or as a patio container plant. Like all crape-myrtle, the dwarf Chickasaw requires full sun.

Chickasaw has the most complicated pedigree of all hybrids introduced to date. It is:
{[**Lagerstroemia indica** dwarf lavender x ((**Lagerstroemia indica** dwarf red x **Lagerstroemia fauriei**) x (**Lagerstroemia indica** dwarf red x **Lagerstroemia fauriei**))] x [(**Lagerstroemia indica** dwarf red x **Lagerstroemia fauriei**) x (**Lagerstroemia indica** Low Flame x **Lagerstroemia fauriei**]} x {[**Lagerstroemia indica** dwarf medium pink x ((**Lagerstroemia indica** dwarf red x **Lagerstroemia fauriei**) x (**Lagerstroemia indica** dwarf red x **Lagerstroemia fauriei**))] x [(**Lagerstroemia indica** dwarf red x **Lagerstroemia fauriei**) x (**Lagerstroemia indica** Low Flame x **Lagerstroemia fauriei**)]}.

Hope

Over time, Hope has failed to measure up to the hopes of those who chose it. This **Lagerstroemia indica** seedling selection has white to very light pink blooms that fade to a paler pink as the flowers age. It is a small plant, slightly looser and taller than Centennial or Victor that were selected from the same group. The lack of a distinctive flower color contributes to the low rating I give it.

Hope was named to honor the city of Hope, Arkansas, the birthplace of President Bill Clinton. It is therefore fitting that these Arkansas selections will be planted on the White House grounds.

These dwarfs could become a new type of bedding plant; perennial, hardy and in less need of attention and care.

If planted in full sun Victor is sure to please!

Ozark Spring

This small, more-upright-than-broad, choice has a light lavender flower show that lasts about 70 days. These blooms fade to almost white as the period extends. As with Hope, this show of color is not outstanding and I rate Ozark Spring on the second level. Although this variety seems to have an early dormancy, we have seen evidence of frost damage in the fall. Dr. Einert wanted to name this cultivar Otto Spring, in honor of the early crapemyrtle grower. Dr. Donald Egolf, then the registrar for **Lagerstroemia**, preferred names with more universal connotation, not the names of living persons, so we got Ozark Spring.

Victor

Through the years, I have enjoyed Victor as much as any other **Lagerstroemia indica**. After the worst winters, Victor performed like the champion it is. The deep red flowers, as red as any crapemyrtle, last for about 85 days. This compact rounded plant begins flowering in late June in north Alabama and shines throughout the summer.

Realizing we had a special cultivar, we put extra effort into introducing and selling Victor to our grower customers. Sales began slowly. Only a few saw the potential of this small crapemyrtle. It has now become one of the most requested varieties on our list.

Victor was named to honor Dr. Victor Watts, a co-developer of these four crapemyrtle. He held emeritus status at the time of these releases. Some of the best beds of massed Victor I have seen are on the campus of Mississippi State University in Starkville, Mississippi, and in downtown Memphis, Tennessee. And, as a statement to its hardiness, Barry Turner has had good success with Victor in New York City.

Turner manages the private Hudson View Gardens in upper Manhattan. There, Victor has grown and flowered beautifully for several years, although an especially hard winter did require replacement. The small amount of money invested in the original plants paid great dividends.

Victor should grow to about four feet if given adequate space. When these crapemyrtle are crowded, they may reach five or six feet. If planted in full sun, this one is sure to please!

Velma's Royal Delight

This exciting new crapemyrtle was introduced in 1991 by Dr. John Pair, a research horticulturist from Kansas State University. It was selected by Mrs. Velma McDaniel of Wichita, Kansas as a chance **Lagerstroemia indica** seedling which came originally from the Otto Spring Nursery at Okmulgee, Oklahoma. We have been involved in growing and evaluating it since 1990.

Here's what I *know*. The superb magenta (or "dazzling purple" as John Pair describes it) flowers occur in mid-summer for about 70 to 85 days. It is slow-growing, dense, strong, able to support its blooms, and relatively free of trouble from insects and diseases.

Dr. Pair reports that Velma's survived -18°F, on December 22, 1989, in Wichita, Kansas. **Nandina domestica**, nearby, was injured worse. Although the top was damaged, the re-growth from the base was excellent and the plants flowered beautifully in summer 1990. In the same shrub evaluation, other **Lagerstroemia indica**s—Centennial Spirit, Natchez, Hardy Lavender, Prairie Lace, and Royalty—were completely killed. Dr. Pair believes Velma's to be distinctly superior.

Velma McDaniel, a Kansas crapemyrtle enthusiast.

57

Dr. Pair
believes
Velma's
to be
distinctly
superior.

Here's what I *think*: Velma's will grow to about five feet tall and four feet wide. It may provide the genetic material necessary to greatly broaden the effective geographic range for **Lagerstroemia**. Velma's has been provided to the National Arboretum for further evaluation and any use they wish. Kansas State University, Dr. Pair and Mrs. McDaniel should get a blue ribbon for this superb cultivar!

We must mention one more group of **Lagerstroemia**, called "miniature weeping crapemyrtle." These are very small-growing plants. Few grow larger than five feet tall, although we have seen some up to six or seven feet in field plantings. These are best when used in hanging baskets or massed as perennial bedding plants. In some ways, they are superior to ordinary bedding plants, in that they bloom for over 100 days, regularly survive normal winters, and flourish in the hottest summers.

David Chopin told me he began a selection process with seedlings from USDA dwarf crapemyrtle (I don't know what these might be). He worked through several generations, and chose those with weeping, open habits, emphasizing self-branching and lateral spread. The selected plants were offered in the late 1970s by Chopin and Wright Nurseries of Baton Rouge, Louisiana.

One of these miniature weeping crapemyrtle was selected to be the official plant of the 1984 Louisiana World's Fair in New Orleans. Interest was created when between four and five thousand were planted. The large masses, in strategic locations, showed them off to their best advantage.

All of these cultivars are patented, making it illegal for unlicensed growers to propagate them for sale without prior arrangements with Mr. Chopin, now of Washington, Pennsylvania. I have had no experience with these miniature selections, so this information is provided by the developer, David Chopin. The varieties are each described as follows:

BATON ROUGE – Early bright red flowers, heavy bloomer, still the most popular landscaping variety. May reach three feet tall.

BAYOU MARIE – The flowers are pink with a deep red edging along the outside of the petal, more apparent in cooler weather. Beautiful grey-green foliage. Grows to three feet.

BI-COLOR – Each of the flowers on this new variety is mixed, red and white. With an upright habit, it is excellent as a specimen in a landscape planting. May reach four and a half feet in height.

BOURBON STREET – Watermelon red flowers, heavy bloomer. Two feet is the expected ultimate height.

CHISAM FIRE – This new selection has bright-red flowers, upright habit and is an especially heavy bloomer. Sometimes grows to four and one-half feet.

CORDON BLEU – Heavy flowers of lavender-blue. Grows to three feet.

CREOLE – The layered habit and watermelon flowers make this one a favorite. Will usually reach three feet. Looks great in half barrels or other large containers.

DELTA BLUSH – Blooms early and regularly with pink flowers. Grows to 18 inches high.

HOUSTON – A seedling from the popular World's Fair variety. It has a full symmetrical habit, and grows to about 24 inches. Attractive watermelon-red flowers.

LAFAYETTE – This selection has an unusual lavender-white flower, and an upright growth habit. May grow to 18 inches.

MARDI GRAS – Chopin describes this upright, then cascading habit, as "oval-weeping." It has purple flowers and grows to three feet high.

NEW ORLEANS – This purple flowering variety grows to only 12 inches, making it the smallest of this group.

PINK BLUSH – This new selection is unusual because of its narrow, compound, grey-green foliage, resembling that of a Nandina. It flowers with a bright-pink bloom and may grow to 18 inches.

*Crapemyrtlettes
are usually
a disappointment.*

PIXIE WHITE - Lots of pure white flowers appear on this 24-inch plant.

PURPLE VELVET - This choice has very different, dark purple flowers, and grows to about four and one-half feet with an upright habit.

SACRAMENTO - The compact, full, symmetrical habit supports lots of deep-red blooms, with a particularly heavy, second flowering period. It was chosen as a seedling from World's Fair. May reach 24 inches.

WORLD'S FAIR - This is the best all-round selection, bearing deep-red flowers, and growing to about 24 inches. It was featured in large plantings at the New Orleans World Exposition.

Some mail-order catalogs, featuring garden plants and products, have for years offered a product called "crapemyrtlettes." This is a novelty item. The seed delivered to my dad in 1975, and another lot I planted later, both produced a group of tiny crapemyrtle with lots of variety in the color of flowers. We found these to be very susceptible to powdery mildew. For the gardener who wants a real summer show, these will be a disappointment.

Crapemyrtle, Mature Height 5 to 10 Feet

This midsize group of crapemyrtle is my favorite category. Most of these are **Lagerstroemia indica** X **Lagerstroemia fauriei** hybrids which means improved mildew resistance, heavy recurrent flowering, superb exfoliating bark and good winter hardiness. The size range is appropriate for so many different needs; the smaller yards and courts of today's homes, limited planting areas of commercial parking lots, and even planters, provided the container has sufficient soil volume to buffer the roots from winter cold.

Too often we see an unhappy situation in which a large-growing variety is massacred with the pruning saw, to accommodate a place that is perfect for these more reserved growing beauties.

Sioux Crapemyrtle at the Smithsonian in Washington, DC.

Acoma

My love affair with Acoma began during a visit to the National Arboretum. While walking with Dr. Donald Egolf through the impressive garden, we came upon an Acoma planted in a neat bed of decorative bark, surrounded by the green lawn, and displayed against the soft blue background of large **Juniperus** specimens. This Acoma was broad, strong and beautiful.

Usually wider than tall, with a distinctively different growth habit, Acoma belongs on all lists of number-one cultivars. Because of this wide and almost weeping habit, this cultivar will be a stunning choice to grow with a single trunk (a "standard" in the trade), with branching about four feet above the ground.

Acoma delivers white flowers for about 90 days, beginning in late June, and light grey bark which is beautifully exposed by exfoliation as the trunks age.

Caddo Crapemyrtle.

The parents of Acoma are **Lagerstroemia indica** Pink Ruffles and an unnamed seedling cross of **Lagerstroemia indica** and **Lagerstroemia fauriei** selected by Dr. Egolf. Purple-red fall color, high mildew resistance, and a 90-day blooming period are special attributes of this splendid small tree. In our nursery and at the National Arboretum, Acoma has been proven to be very winter hardy.

Be sure and try this one. Acoma is a plant for everyone.

Caddo

This is another nice, pink crapemyrtle. This cultivar came from a 1965 National Arboretum cross of **Lagerstroemia indica** X **fauriei** Basham's Party Pink and **Lagerstroemia indica** Cherokee. Its spreading, multi-stemmed habit and bright pink flowers are very pretty. Blooms begin in mid-July and last for about 80 days.

Often we hear that there are just too many crapemyrtle choices, especially pink choices. This selection began badly because of a limited distribution. There was good reason for this; Caddo is difficult to root. Few crapemyrtle give trouble in the propagating bed. Why spend time with one that does, especially when there is no great difference between it and several other cultivars?

I hate to black-list any of the hybrids that were judged to pass during the complete screening and evaluation at the National Arboretum, but I really think we have several pink flowering crapemyrtle at least as good as Caddo.

Cherokee

This **Lagerstroemia indica** was introduced by the National Arboretum in 1970. It was the only red-flowering cultivar from the early work, before the hybrids came along, that passed all tests and was released. Unfortunately, the distribution to the evaluators and propagating nurseries was mixed with other unknown seedlings. This choice never got a fair chance to show its stuff. Several nurseries have continued growing and selling these plants, listing and picturing them in their catalogs, thus causing plenty of confusion in the trade. Attempting to grow the real Cherokee, I ordered them several times, from several nurseries, and each time received mixed or improperly labeled plants.

Finally I went to the National Arboretum to take cuttings from the original plant. It has a compact, medium growth habit, and blooms from July through September. **Lagerstroemia indica** hardy red and **Lagerstroemia indica** Low Flame were crossed to give Cherokee.

Now that we have Tonto, Cherokee will likely fade from use. This selection could have been a fine addition to the list in 1970, but now adds little.

Hopi

This National Arboretum hybrid is a five-star favorite. The low shrubby habit is a perfect support for displaying the profusion of recurring, superior-pink flowers. Usually growing to about one and one-half times wide as high, Hopi is effectively used in masses, low and spectacular hedges, or in planters.

In the initial trials in Washington, DC, winter observations demonstrated that Hopi was very hardy; in fact, Hopi, introduced in 1986, is the most hardy of all the mid-size group. But even if it is winter killed, a heavy pruning (to the ground) will bring about re-growth and the wonderful summer display of blooms.

Hopi, whose parents are (**Lagerstroemia indica** Pink Lace X **Lagerstroemia fauriei**) X **Lagerstroemia indica** Alba Nana, has all the best attributes of these new hybrids: high mildew resistance, about 100 days of recurrent flowering, great exfoliating bark, and splendid orange-red fall color. A note of caution: tiny, iridescent-green flea beetles love this cultivar. Like all crapemyrtle, Hopi does its best work in full sun.

Pecos

The pretty medium-pink flowers of Pecos are usually the first crapemyrtle blooms to be seen at our farm each year. It grows as a leggy, semi-dwarf shrub to about eight feet tall and six feet wide. The special features expected on a National Arboretum hybrid are all present. Pecos is mildew-resistant. The trunk bark has dark brown colors after exfoliation. It can be expected to flower for about 100 days each summer.

A field of crapemyrtle.

Dr. Egolf selected this choice from seedlings from a cross of [**Lagerstroemia indica** dwarf red X **Lagerstroemia fauriei**] X [**Lagerstroemia indica** dark red X **Lagerstroemia fauriei**] that was made in 1972. Pecos was introduced in 1986.

Pecos has never been one of my favorites. I dislike its habit of growth when it is young. But as I have seen more mature plants, I have re-evaluated my first impressions. There is a place for this first-flowering, pink crapemyrtle.

Prairie Lace

While at Oklahoma State, Dr. Carl Whitcomb developed two new (and I do mean new!) **Lagerstroemia indica**. The reason I emphasize the new is his method of treating the seed before planting.

All of the very early named varieties of crapemyrtle were simple selections made from open pollinated seed, usually in a nursery setting, not from controlled laboratory work or an experimental plot. Whitcomb treated a group of seed with a four percent solution of ethylmethane sulfonate (a compound with the ability to play genetic games), put the resulting seedlings through a rigorous selection process, then made choices. (Whitcomb cautions, "Mentioning this compound may encourage others to try it without knowing the hazards. EMS is *very* toxic, nasty to handle and a *strong* carcinogen!") Prairie Lace is a result of that work. It was introduced in 1984. It is not certain that this choice is a mutant; maybe it's just a lucky find.

This cultivar was selected for mildew resistance, good form and flowering characteristics. And the flowers really are worth notice, performing for about 100 days. The individual petals are medium pink, banded by pure white on the outer margin. Probably because of the mutant origin, few viable seed are produced by these blooms. Prairie Lace has good winter hardiness and remarkable foliage color. New leaves emerge burgundy-red and mature to very dark green, later changing to a red fall color. The habit of growth is a compact upright shrub.

I have never been a strong advocate for two-toned flowers on crapemyrtle. Some larger growers chose to patent, name, and publicize early selections that are common in the trade. These rugged plants are much more effective when blasting out the dominating major colors than when dancing around pretending to be petunias.

One other concern: when Dr. Whitcomb left the University to begin his private consulting work, the question arose—to patent or not to patent. Restricting propagation rights on new plants, arising from their research work, is a scheme currently used by some universities to augment their funding. An extended period of indecision ended with a plan to patent which limited production, increased paperwork, and negatively affected the popularity of this cultivar.

Tonto

A major shortcoming of Dr. Donald Egolf's early crapemyrtle breeding program at the National Arboretum was the lack of deep red flowers on any of the cultivars that included **Lagerstroemia fauriei** in their parentage. When he introduced Tonto in 1990, that gap was filled. Bright red florets displayed against the dark green foliage and the fine mounding, multi-stemmed habit, cause this to be a blue-ribbon cultivar.

This choice grew to about eight and one-half feet high and wide in 15 years. Probably it will mature as a bit more upright plant. In Florida and coastal areas, growers expect Tonto to grow larger than the ten feet this group might indicate. Its uses, like most of those in this size group, include informal hedges, low screens, small specimen trees, and even large containers for patios and courtyards. And as with others in this size, the exfoliating bark is good but not as effective as in the larger growing cultivars.

Tonto, which was selected as a Georgia Gold Medal Winner in 1996, has high mildew resistance and very good winter hardiness. A 1995 study reported by the Louisiana Agricultural Extension Service indicated that—out of thirty-four varieties— Tonto had the greatest resistance to both leaf spot diseases and early fall defoliation. Crossing of [(**Lagerstroemia indica** Pink Lace X **Lagerstroemia fauriei**) X **Lagerstroemia indica** Catawba] X **Lagerstroemia indica** Tuscarora, as an attempt to intensify flower color and mildew resistance, resulted in this selection.

Zuni makes a neat and lovely small tree.
(Photo credit to U.S. National Arboretum, Washington, DC)

Tonto will be a near-trouble-free favorite for those who enjoy the slower, more controlled growth and the heavy, recurrent, fuchsia flowering show. Some growers have chosen Tonto as their main red variety, but I am concerned with the slower rate of growth and their need for rapid production. Also we find Tonto to be one of the more hesitant cultivars to produce roots in the propagation bed. It is certain to be among the best reds, especially for container production.

Zuni

Zuni has very pretty medium to dark lavender flowers. Several of the Indian tribe cultivars have soft lavender blooms, so this deeper color is quite welcome. Because of recurrent flowering, the period begins in late June and lasts up to 100 days, but perhaps the quantity of flowers is a bit less than others in this group. However, I feel Zuni will prove to be one of the lasting choices from the work at the National Arboretum.

The dark green foliage seems to have a leathery look, and in the fall an outstanding orange-red foliage color. The parents of Zuni, [**Lagerstroemia indica** dwarf red X **Lagerstroemia fauriei**] X **Lagerstroemia indica** Low Flame, were crossed in 1972 and the introduction was made in 1986.

This choice has strong mildew resistance, exfoliating bark, and good winter hardiness. Its adaptable, multi-use form is a small upright tree with some spreading limbs. Light annual pruning can maintain the appearance necessary for low hedges or masses. Occasional hard pruning to the ground will invigorate and thicken the plant, causing increased flowering on the new growth that occurs.

Crapemyrtle, Mature Height Ten To Twenty Feet

When I say the mature height of this group is ten to twenty feet, you must know that is our best guess. Crapemyrtle often grow in a fashion defined by the environment provided. I have observed Tuskegee, which is among those with the broadest habit of growth, at near thirty feet tall while only about five feet wide. This anomaly was caused by crowded and uncomfortable surroundings not found in normal plantings. After we have grown these crapemyrtle for about fifty years, we will know as a fact the proper mature size for each.

Apalachee

Dr. Donald Egolf had, just as we all do, his own personal biases. He expressed to me several times his special feeling that Apalachee was a splendid choice. I disagreed at first, but after watching for about ten years, I now wholeheartedly agree.

This cultivar has lots of neat, compact, six- to eight-inch, light-lavender flowers performing for about 90 days every summer beginning in June. It resulted from the cross of **Lagerstroemia indica** Azuka Dwarf Hybrid X **Lagerstroemia fauriei** and was introduced to the trade in 1987. It grows to be an attractive, upright, multi-stemmed, small tree.

Apalachee is hardy, has good mildew resistance, and is a wonderful tree. As did most trees of this size range, Apalachee withstood -23° C (convert that to about -9° F) in Washington, DC, with little or no damage. Its very dark green summer leaves, russet fall foliage color and superb display of cinnamon to chestnut-brown exfoliating bark, put Apalachee on the sure-to-succeed list. An additional feature is the golden beauty of the dried flower heads after the seed have fallen.

Lavender often is not the color of first choice in crapemyrtle or many other things. I think Apalachee will help us overcome this prejudice. So many fall into the habit of selecting only red or pink for flower displays. Being no color expert (my wife suggests I sidestep all color discussions), I fail to understand the thinking of those who avoid the unusual. The cool effect of the soft lavender flowers of this cultivar is just what I'd like near my late afternoon chair on the patio.

On a cloudy, dark day in Washington, I visited the National Arboretum. I had planned to photograph crapemyrtle flowers for this book, but there wasn't enough light to work. Still I was so glad to be there that stormy day, to see Apalachee's scintillating performance. In the gardens that included crapemyrtle of many colors, I saw the flowers of Apalachee give off a bright, soft light, clearly standing out among all the others. The glow from these blooms was what really attracted attention in this planting. This is a special choice.

Catawba

One of the first four **Lagerstroemia indica** cultivars to receive the American Indian name (which indicates it is from Egolf's work at the National Arboretum in Washington, DC), Catawba is a marvelous 1967 introduction. It resulted from a cross of **Lagerstroemia indica** dwarf purple X **Lagerstroemia indica** light lavender.

High mildew resistance and red-orange fall color are important attributes, but the real reason for celebration is Catawba's violet-purple flowers. Many Southern landscape architects have realized that Catawba will give them the old-fashioned crapemyrtle look in a new high-performance style.

Other and older **Lagerstroemia indica** with similar flower color completely failed both the

mildew resistance and winter hardiness tests, making Catawba a welcome addition to the list of choices. The exhibition of bark colors is somewhat limited in **Lagerstroemia indica**. That is not so important in the shorter growing plants, since there is less stem and trunk to parade that display. I've seen no Catawba larger than about 12 feet high, so it is smaller than most in this group. It is the best dark purple bloomer in our list.

Centennial Spirit

While Dr. Carl Whitcomb was teaching at Oklahoma State University, he began working with chemical treatments of crapemyrtle seed, attempting to make improved selections of seedlings from mutation breeding (see Prairie Lace). Centennial Spirit is a second-generation product of that work; it is a natural cross of one of those seedlings with a normal **Lagerstroemia indica**. It was introduced in 1984.

The primary feature of this impressive cultivar is the magnificent electric red flowers which, unlike those of most crapemyrtle, do not fade with age. The oldest blooms seem to have the same intensity of color as the newest flowers. Viable seed are produced. Centennial Spirit is an upright, multi-stemmed tree with reduced tendencies to suckering, which is a common problem for many varieties. Of all cultivars tested in Florida trials, Centennial Spirit is the least susceptible to aphids.

This vigorous crapemyrtle offers some mildew resistance, good winter hardiness, and fine red-orange fall foliage tones.

About this stout cultivar, Whitcomb said, "The large upright inflorescences appear much like a torch with a strong handle, thus the name "Centennial Spirit." Although I am troubled by the plant patent problem and subsequent decisions by Oklahoma

Crapemyrtle, Mature Height 10 to 20 Feet Tall

Seminole Crapemyrtle

Tuskegee Crapemyrtle

Apalachee Crapemyrtle

Sioux Crapemyrtle

10 to 20 Feet Tall

70

Sioux Crapemyrtle

Conestoga Crapemyrtle

10 to 20 Feet Tall

10 to 20 Feet Tall

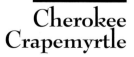

Regal Red
Crapemyrtle

Cherokee
Crapemyrtle

Comanche Crapemyrtle

Centennial Spirit
Crapemyrtle

10 to 20 Feet Tall

Yuma Crapemyrtle

Raspberry Sundae
Crapemyrtle

Osage Crapemyrtle

Catawba Crapemyrtle

10 to 20 Feet Tall

10 to 20 Feet Tall

Lipan Crapemyrtle

Powhatan Crapemyrtle

State University to require payment for production of this cultivar, I feel we need to place this one with our first level.

And Whitcomb's work continues. He is seeking the perfect white crapemyrtle and has interest in any new seedlings that add to our currently available colors, and levels of disease resistance and hardiness.

Comanche

This pleasant National Arboretum hybrid has pink flowers with an added orange tone. (My wife, Janie, forbids me to call the color coral, although others may do so!) Blooming begins in July and continues till September.

Its habit is generally upright with a broad spreading crown. It exhibits medium vigor, meaning fairly slow growth.

Comanche has an excellent sandalwood inner bark when the exfoliation occurs in the late summer. Special features are good mildew resistance and impressive, deep red-purple fall foliage color. I like the strong and hardy character of this selection.

Comanche has been selected by landscape architect Mike Donnelly, of Huntsville, Alabama, for use on interstate highway plantings. Some have called crapemyrtle a "60 mile-per-hour" plant, meaning the flowering is effective when viewed at that speed. This requires strong bloom color and large masses. Stringing a few plants here and there will not show these beauties at their best. Plantings along the Georgia highways, installed in 1995, demonstrate clearly the value of large groups during the flowering period.

Parents of Comanche are **Lagerstroemia indica** dark red X (**Lagerstroemia indica** X **Lagerstroemia fauriei** seedling). It was bred in 1969, selected in 1973 and introduced in 1987.

Crapemyrtle is a "60 mile-per-hour" plant, meaning the flowering is effective when viewed at that speed.

Conestoga

Conestoga, another of the first four **Lagerstroemia indica** selections from the National Arboretum, has several unusual characteristics. Abundant, long, tapered flowers of light lavender color attract attention. The broad, open, pendulous growth habit is accentuated by the terminal positioning and size of the blooms. This is especially true when rain adds weight to those blooms, often causing them to bow to the ground. As with most pure **Lagerstroemia indica**, the bark lacks the exfoliating beauty of the hybrids.

Conestoga is used as a primary street tree in several cities, including Auburn, Alabama, and Sarasota, Florida. Special pruning or support is necessary to allow these crapemyrtle to perform well in areas near vehicle and pedestrian traffic because of the semi-weeping form.

Conestoga resulted from Dr. Egolf's cross of **Lagerstroemia indica** white X **Lagerstroemia indica** Low Flame and was released in 1966. Although it is easy to grow and sure to flower, a slight susceptibility to powdery mildew and the arching habit limit the usefulness of this cultivar.

Dynamite

When Dr. Carl Whitcomb was walking through a block of new crapemyrtle seedlings, he came upon this one. In his words, he said, "Wow, this one is Dynamite!" **Lagerstroemia indica** Whit II was selected and named at his Stillwater, Oklahoma research farm.

The crimson flower buds become cherry red blooms and are set against a background of thick, green, leathery leaves which start as crimson-toned young foliage. This cultivar roots and transplants with great ease. It is a vigorous, upright grower and, in the right location, may reach twenty feet tall. So far, it has withstood winter cold to -5° F. As crapemyrtle age, their tolerance for winter increases, especially if pruning, fertilizing and watering do not increase juvenility.

Dynamite will be restricted to licensed propagators since it will hold a plant patent and the name "Dynamite" is trademarked. It is from the same parentage as other Whitcomb selections, Raspberry Sundae and Centennial Spirit, only several generations down the line.

Lipan

One of the problems in naming plants with unusual proper nouns is pronunciation. It is debatable whether Lipan is pronounced "Li-PAN'" or "LIP-an." Either way, this is one exceptional crapemyrtle. A special feature is the white, (yes, white!) layer of bark, exposed in the late summer by exfoliation of older plants. A Sycamore tree has more bark to show, but this crapemyrtle display can bring a similar exhibit to many more home and community gardens.

When one regularly walks through fields of these lovelies, it is easy to begin thinking of and classifying them as people. In my mind I can easily see Lipan as a beautiful woman, with erect posture, dressed in a fashionable business suit and high-heeled shoes. Crazy? Sure. But I *really* like this crapemyrtle.

The fashionable purplish-lavender flowers are borne on a broad, upright habit of growth. This is a beautiful, cold-hardy, small tree. Because Lipan's parents are (**Lagerstroemia indica** Pink Lace X **Lagerstroemia fauriei**) X [(**Lagerstroemia indica** red X **Lagerstroemia indica** Carolina Beauty) X **Lagerstroemia indica** X **fauriei** Bashams's Party

Pink], it is highly resistant to mildew. The Georgia Plant Selections Committee put Lipan on their Gold Medal Winner list in 1996.

Near East

If a beautiful flower was the only requirement for membership in the Crapemyrtle Hall of Fame, Near East would have a front row seat at the banquet. The tones of the soft pink bloom are superb. In other areas the plant completely fails. The rounded, open-spreading habit of growth is fine but the seriously brittle limbs have lots of breakage when handled. Probably this cultivar has the least ability to tolerate winter cold of all the **Lagerstroemia indica** we have ever grown. In our north Alabama location, damage occurs almost every year. Farther south, Near East can serve satisfactorily. Old plantings at the entrance to Callaway Gardens in south central Georgia were magnificent for years.

It is thought this cultivar was brought from Eastern Asia in about 1870, subsequently was lost to the trade, then it was given to Kay Sawada of Overlook Nurseries in Mobile, Alabama, by Mrs. D. Debaillon of Washington, Louisiana. He named and introduced it in 1952. Near East has fair mildew resistance but a 1994 Louisiana study lists it as highly susceptible to a leaf spot fungal organism called **Cercospora lythracearum**.

Osage

I really like Osage. For several years, I've thought that this selection should be named "Wal-Mart." Its loud, showy, billboard-like appearance is quite an imposing feature in a landscape planting. The habit is open, rounding and slightly pendulous. The form and the very heavy flowering pattern cause

Osage Crapemyrtle

The loud, showy, billboard-like appearance of Osage is quite an imposing feature in a landscape planting.

me to imagine a fat smiling statue of Buddha, occupying a lot of room. Clear-pink blooms, in great numbers, appear from late June through September, and then the show continues with red fall foliage coloring.

Every year, I forget how pretty the Osage flowers are. When a few show up in mid-June I am happily amazed.

I think Osage is best used when massed on the corners of large buildings or grouped in lawns or roadsides where a big splash of color is needed. The chestnut brown bark is one more good feature.

Dr. Egolf selected Osage from a group of seedlings hybridized from [**Lagerstroemia indica** dwarf red X **Lagerstroemia fauriei**] X [**Lagerstroemia indica** Pink Lace X **Lagerstroemia fauriei**] in 1976 and it was named and introduced in 1987. Good winter hardiness and mildew resistance add to the glory of Osage.

Powhatan

This cultivar originated from the same cross—**Lagerstroemia indica** dwarf purple X **Lagerstroemia indica** light lavender—as the previously-mentioned Catawba. In some ways the two are similar. The principal differences are that Powhatan grows a bit larger, grows more quickly, and the color of its medium to dark-purple flower is slightly less intense. In the autumn the difference is obvious: Catawba has orange-red leaf colors while Powhatan exhibits clear yellow tones. Although this cultivar has no **fauriei** genes, it has good mildew tolerance and the ability to withstand cold weather.

An excellent specimen of Powhatan is growing in the bonsai area of the National Arboretum in Washington. Dr. Marc Cathey, former director of the Arboretum, pointed out to me the results of gentle pruning and its effect on the natural form of this example. Each trunk was allowed to grow on and up without topping while allowing for natural side branching. This is the true way for a crapemyrtle to live its life. Powhatan has never been in large supply in the industry, but serves well when chosen for lawns and gardens. It was one of the early **Lagerstroemia indica** selections from the Egolf work, which he introduced in 1967.

Raspberry Sundae

This is one more cultivar from the ongoing work of Dr. Carl Whitcomb. It is an exceptional choice because of habit, foliage color and especially the flower. Each bloom is pinkish-red with a white edge, from which the name "sundae" comes—you can just see the whipped cream topping. In full sun and hot summer days, the variegated flowers tend to be more red than pink. The dark burgundy foliage is a traffic stopper and the habit is tall and columnar, much like a **Quercus robur fastigata**, but a bit wider at the base.

Whitcomb says he has found terminal cuttings more often grow a plant with a central leader. If this proves out, we may have a wonderful cultivar to more easily grow as a standard or single-trunk tree.

We have grown Raspberry Sundae on trial for several years and it is really a different selection. We have observed a bit of powdery mildew in our North Alabama nursery, while at locations in Oklahoma and Florida, Raspberry Sundae has been absolutely mildew free. I feel this will only be a minor problem. The outstanding form and features will outweigh a bit of mildew. It blooms heavily in the hottest years. I'm told that the Florida growers love Raspberry Sundae.

It will grow to about fifteen feet tall and has been exposed to -5° F winter cold with hardly any damage. Like most crapemyrtle it roots and transplants very easily.

Whitcomb named it **Lagerstroemia indica** Whit I and added the trademarked name "Raspberry Sundae." This addition to the crapemyrtle world was patented and introduced in 1996.

Regal Red

My father, Marcus D. Byers, had a lifelong interest in all plants. He loved collecting and planting seed and spent untold hours evaluating the results. He chose a number of hollies, dogwood, and crapemyrtle. **Lagerstroemia indica** Regal Red is one of those.

Regal Red caught his eye because of one outstanding attribute: its vivid red flower color. I think only Carolina Beauty comes close to Regal Red in fine, real-red blooms. Regal Red has a broadly upright form with a rounded head and barely makes this 10 to 20 foot size group. As I look from our office now, the original plant is only 12 feet tall after 25 years of growing at our office site. It was frozen and killed to the ground in the -16° F weather on Christmas eve, 1983, and -15° F in January, 1985, but recovered and quickly became an effective plant again.

Recurrent flowering, good mildew resistance and hardiness in normal winters make this one of the few really good, dark red crapemyrtle for all the South. Its early and heavy flowering pattern make Regal Red a favorite for container growers. Red-orange fall leaves are a continuing part of its display.

Regal Red Crapemyrtle at Mississsppi State University.

81

Royal Velvet

The newest cultivar from the productive work of Dr. Carl Whitcomb is this drought-tolerant, vigorous-growing choice. He describes it as a large multiple-stem shrub that has proven winter hardy to -5° F in Oklahoma. **Lagerstroemia indica** Whit III is available now only to licensed growers, because he has applied for a patent. The name "Royal Velvet" is trademarked.

The burgundy new growth slowly fades to purplish green. Flowering begins with crimson buds opening to bright pink flowers early in the summer. We have not yet tried this selection in Alabama, but if it is as good as the earlier crapemyrtle Whitcomb has put into American gardens, it will be wonderful.

Seminole

This fine flowering crapemyrtle just slipped from sight as other cultivars were introduced. The very early, large, clear-pink blooms are the outstanding feature of Seminole. I have often recommended this choice for those finishing plants in large containers. It has a dense, globose habit, strong enough to support the sizable blooms. If grown in a #10 container, this plant can grow to five feet wide and high and give a circus of color, consistently flowering with recurrent bloom, late in the season. I have seen these flowers as fat as a 15-inch bucket!

Dr. Egolf introduced this **Lagerstroemia indica** in 1970. Parents of Seminole are **Lagerstroemia indica** hardy pink X **Lagerstroemia indica** Low Flame. It is tolerant of mildew but may show a slight infection in late season. The round dark green leaves and dense appearance give the feel of heavy texture on this highly ornamental plant.

Seminole has good ability to withstand the challenges of winter and the yellow fall foliage adds to this desirable package. Its ultimate height just barely fits in this over ten foot group.

Sioux

Through the years I have chosen as my favorite several varieties of crapemyrtle. One, then another, would impress me for some reason, and I would proclaim it my favorite. This great cultivar may make my all-time list!

It was easy to know, early on, that Sioux was to be a remarkable selection. When customers rode with me through our fields and trial blocks, most would point toward it and ask for the name. The vivid, shocking-pink flower surely requires 220 volts to perform. A Georgia plant selection committee agrees. This remarkable selection was a Georgia Gold Medal Winner in 1996.

The common worrisome questions are answered with Sioux. In mildew resistance, winter hardiness, and habit, this is a fine plant.

Sioux's exceptional attributes are covered in one word: color. The very-alive pink, recurrent flower displayed against the almost-burgundy foliage is unusual, striking and lasts from late July to mid-September. The majestic maroon fall foliage color is one of its very best attributes.

A group of Sioux was planted in 1994 at the front of the Smithsonian Institute's American History Museum in Washington, DC. As time passes this is sure to be a spectacle of color. Against white or beige buildings, this intense pink on burgundy display will cause comment and bring attention to the landscape.

The late summer exfoliation of the bark produces a show of medium grey brown. Parents of Sioux are [**Lagerstroemia indica** Tiny Fire X

(**Lagerstroemia indica** X **Lagerstroemia fauriei** seedling)] X [**Lagerstroemia indica** Pink Lace X **Lagerstroemia fauriei**) X **Lagerstroemia indica** Catawba].

Tuskegee

Among this palette of many choices we enjoy, unusual form is very important. This selection is different because the habit is the most horizontal of all, when grown with lots of space and sunlight.

Like all crapemyrtle, Tuskegee will adapt to its surroundings; I have seen it grow tall and narrow when squeezed into close spacing.

The normally broad and beautiful, distinctively-horizontal form and dark-pink to red flowers cause this cultivar to score high on our list of all-stars. Tuskegee was given an excellent rating after eight years in a trial planting at Cape Girardeau, Missouri. And at the other crapemyrtle extreme, Florida, this plant is a strong performer.

In 1968, Dr. Egolf hybridized **Lagerstroemia indica** Dallas Red with **Lagerstroemia indica** X **fauriei** Basham's Party Pink. From this backcross, seed were collected, seedlings were grown and observed, and Tuskegee was selected for its exceptional vigor and lustrous green leaves and intense dark pink flowers. Propagation was begun in 1972, distribution for trial and stock increase in 1981 and then in August 1986, publication and introduction in *HortScience*. This typical scenario gives one an idea of the time and work necessary to bring a new cultivar to the gardening world.

Other special features of Tuskegee are about 100 days of flamboyant flowering, superb red-orange fall foliage and its mottled grey-tan exfoliating bark. It is mildew resistant and cold tolerant. Egolf's writings suggest it is best used as an isolated landscape specimen.

The white exfoliating bark of Lipan Crapemyrtle is a remarkable feature (Photo credit to U.S. National Arboretum, Washington, DC)

The right cultivar in its proper place is the highest creative use of our wonderful Lagerstroemia.

William Toovey

This crapemyrtle was first listed in the catalog of Howell Nursery of Knoxville, Tennessee, in 1927. There were only a very few names given to a selection prior to this, except those indicating flower color, such as "red" or "white." This name has been used in an abbreviated manner, Wm. Toovey, in most listings, including *The Lagerstroemia Handbook/Checklist*. I believe the proper spelling is not abbreviated. As proof, I found a 1938 catalog from the Howell Nursery in which the name was spelled out completely.

My father had business dealings with the Howells and I remember them well. They were also involved in selection and naming of several **Cornus florida** varieties. It would be interesting to know more about William Toovey and his connection to the Howells, or the area, or the plant. I asked the Howells, retired Tennessee nurseryman Hoskins Shadow, and Dr. Johanna Shields, head of the history department at University of Alabama, Huntsville, for help. Unfortunately, I can find no one who knows.

This name, William Toovey, has through the years been used to indicate a number of different choices across the South, because it was the first *named* variety. The true William Toovey has pink-red flowers, about the color of the flesh of a watermelon, hence the selection is also known by the additional designation, William Toovey, watermelon-red.

As I write this, we still get orders for William Toovey, and many landscape architects continue to use it regularly. Amazingly, for a very early seedling selection, this plant has good mildew resistance and winter hardiness. It exhibits a broadly-upright habit of growth. Newer cultivars are better choices today, because of the longer flowering periods, improved disease resistance and lovely bark colors.

Yuma

The flower form of Yuma is the first and most noticeable feature of this cultivar. If any crapemyrtle can be said to be double, this is it. Two to three hundred florets, with crinkled petals, form the flower, giving the appearance of fullness. Often, these flowers are closely grouped to give the appearance of a handful of lovely lavender softballs in one bouquet. Yuma was a 1996 Georgia Gold Medal Winner.

Yuma's early habit is dense-branched and globose, but as a mature plant it will have open trunks and a spreading crown. It has good winter hardiness, tolerating with little damage, -23° C (or -9° F) in a Washington, DC winter. Remember that winter hardiness is, to a very large degree, affected by the culture given an individual plant in the summer, just prior to the winter.

This cool beauty with its clustered flowers blooms for about 90 days each summer beginning in late July. The foliage is yellow-orange in the fall. The bark of Yuma becomes sinuous, mottled and light grey as exfoliation occurs on the older branches and trunks.

Yuma resulted from the 1972 hybridization of (**Lagerstroemia indica** Pink Lace X **Lagerstroemia fauriei**) X [**Lagerstroemia amabilis** Makino X (**Lagerstroemia indica** hardy light pink X **Lagerstroemia indica** red)]. **Lagerstroemia amabilis** is a natural hybrid of **Lagerstroemia indica** and **Lagerstroemia subcostata**, occurring in Japan where selections with larger flowers are sometimes cultivated.

Yuma Crapemyrtle

Crapemyrtle Cultivars

85

Crapemyrtle, Mature Height of Twenty Feet or More

Most crapemyrtle planted across the South are from this largest group. There are several reasons for this. The oldest varieties selected through the years by nurserymen and gardeners were chosen as small trees. Few thought of crapemyrtle as shrubs.

Growers appreciate those that reach salable sizes quickly, and not only do Natchez and Biloxi do that, but they offer great flowers and beautiful bark. These tallest plants deliver all colors of flowers: deep-red, pink, fine whites and lavenders.

Landscape architects and growers have been slow to try the smaller cultivars, but the future will bring use of all sizes, tall and short, chosen to fit their place perfectly. The right cultivar in its proper place is the highest creative use of our wonderful **Lagerstroemia**.

Basham's Party Pink

If you ask about a large crapemyrtle in Texas, you'll be told about this fast growing variety. In the milder parts of the South, we may see this tree grow to fifty feet tall and thirty-five feet wide. But in the more northern crapemyrtle territories, it will freeze every year.

Apparently an open-pollinated chance seedling, from a cross of **Lagerstroemia indica** and one of the first distributed **Lagerstroemia fauriei**, it was noticed in 1963 and named in 1965 by B. M. Basham, of Conroe, Texas. It was introduced to the trade by Lynn Lowrey, a Texas nurseryman, in 1965.

Basham's Party Pink has many of the features of **Lagerstroemia fauriei**: the vigorous growth, upright habit, with a broad-spreading crown, the large, light-green, sharply-pointed leaves, beautiful exfoliating bark, and the vivid, orange-red to yellow, fall foliage color. The soft lavender-pink blooms are 12 or more inches long and six to eight inches wide, usually appearing in late June.

In many ways, this selection favors Muskogee, an early hybrid cultivar from the National Arboretum, and for most purposes and locations, Muskogee would be the better choice. They are difficult to tell apart until a hard freeze. Still, in the Houston, Texas climate, Basham's discovery is doing a great job. It has good mildew resistance and is very easy to transplant.

Biloxi

The largest Biloxi I have seen is at my back door. I planted it in 1987 and today it is over 30 feet high and 12 feet wide. It would be wider if it were in full sun, rather than in a situation where its light is restricted by the house and nearby trees. The caliper of the largest of the trunks is four to five inches at breast height. The size of this Biloxi might be smaller though, if the wind break and winter protection provided by the house were not in place. Always remember, these crapemyrtle do their very best in full sun!

The vigor of this cultivar is amazing. I believe it is the fastest growing of all those discussed in this book. Pale-pink flowers begin in mid-July and their effectiveness continues for about 80 days. The late July exfoliation of bark reveals beautiful, mottled, dark brown colors; this splendid display alone is a good reason to plant Biloxi. Florida customers report this choice may be their favorite crapemyrtle.

Biloxi was produced by a 1972 cross of [**Lagerstroemia indica** dwarf red X **Lagerstroemia fauriei**] X [**Lagerstroemia indica** Low Flame X **Lagerstroemia fauriei**]. It has excellent powdery mildew resistance and good winter hardiness. The fast-growing nature of this cultivar produces so much soft tissue so fast, that we often see unhealthy levels of aphids and sooty mold. A bit of

attention to that problem will be rewarded with a large and beautiful crapemyrtle, doing what crapemyrtle do best.

Byers Hardy Lavender

For those early crapemyrtle enthusiasts, winter hardiness was the one primary attribute that controlled marketing success. Even as much as flower color, the ability to avoid cold damage was important. This **Lagerstroemia indica** selection was made by my father, Marcus D. Byers, and Ollie Fraser from a group of seedlings at Fraser Nurseries in Birmingham, Alabama in the 1950s.

Hardy Lavender has several fine features, including its outstanding winter hardiness. The soft, medium-lavender flowers begin later than most other crapemyrtle varieties, and that wonderful color punctuates the landscape while most other summer blooms are fading. The 75-day blooming period is effective until frost. This is followed by an energetic, red fall foliage display.

The habit is that of an upright tree with a spreading top. This variety has been regularly used throughout the South and many fine specimens are maturing now. Scores are growing in Memphis, Tennessee and in our city of Huntsville, Alabama. The best Hardy Lavender I have seen are at a McDonald's Restaurant in Starkville, Mississippi, where they were planted by the late Denny Phillips, a local landscape architect. Other wonderful plantings can be seen in Huntsville where George Bennett's award-winning Burger King work includes lots of these beauties.

Byers Standard Red

The lovely soft-red flower of this **Lagerstroemia indica** was the principal reason for its selection, by Marcus D. Byers, from our nursery fields, in Madison County, Alabama, in 1965. This plant grows in an upright vase-shaped form, to about 20 feet high. For a chance seedling, it has good mildew resistance and winter hardiness.

Seventy-five days of flowering, beginning in mid-July, and impressive orange fall foliage color, give the gardener full value for his effort. Other red blooming crapemyrtle may replace our Standard Red, but when used, its performance will be pleasing.

Byers Wonderful White

This superb crapemyrtle has been the criterion for white flowering varieties in the South for many years. Chosen by my father, Marcus D. Byers, Wonderful White has passed the tough tests of bloom quality, winter hardiness, and mildew and insect resistance.

Some years ago, Johnny Brailsford, of Shady Grove Nursery in South Carolina, a trend-setting tree grower of great renown, said to me, "If you don't name and promote this one, I will." With this urging, in 1970, I chose the name and began promoting this variety.

This **Lagerstroemia indica** has several outstanding features that attract attention. First the flower; calling it large isn't doing justice to its size. Many of these flower heads are larger than a basketball. Some years ago I used a photo of my son, Marc, in our sales catalog, holding a flower and a basketball to demonstrate its large size. Its color is a clear white, without the yellow tinges some other white varieties

exhibit. These flowers are displayed on a tall and strong but willowy habit. Wonderful White may have slightly smaller trunk caliper than the norm. This plant's form is broadly upright. The shape may be temporarily altered when the big flowers are weighted by water, after rainfall or irrigation, causing the limbs to bow toward the ground. Fall foliage is a bright yellow display.

Of all the **Lagerstroemia** varieties we have ever grown, Byers Wonderful White has proven the most winter hardy. On only one occasion, following the extreme cold of December 1983, were we required to cut this variety all the way back to the ground. Perhaps we have grown them lean and hungry, predisposing them to better withstand cold winter threats. But when all things are evaluated, this is really a hardy cultivar.

If the crapemyrtle breeding program at the National Arboretum is ever again fully funded, allowing the work to regain momentum, the hardiness of Wonderful White should be included in some of the hybridization work.

Carolina Beauty

We have only a few intensely dark red flowering crapemyrtle and Carolina Beauty is at the top of that list. The depth of this red color is shared with Regal Red and maybe Dallas Red, but none of the fancy hybrids from the National Arboretum work come close to the intensity of this shade.

Carolina Beauty was selected from **Lagerstroemia indica** seedlings in 1940 and named and introduced by the Daily's Nursery of Clinton, South Carolina. This crapemyrtle has been in great demand by landscape professionals across the South for many years. The flower color is an important part of that interest, and the very tall and upright habit is another hallmark. A distinguishing feature of Carolina Beauty is a different and extreme, upright trunk pattern. The almost parallel nature of the trunk structure is unusual, and I have seen it in no other crapemyrtle.

The use of this selection will decrease in the future, because of an unfortunate attraction for aphids and powdery mildew. We see that all sizes and ages of Carolina Beauty have little to no resistance to disease, but if there is an absolute requirement for a tall, dark red crapemyrtle, then this cultivar is the only choice.

Choctaw

Dr. Egolf commented that this may be the finest tree cultivar yet! It is still too soon to be sure about that. Some have suggested Choctaw is a pink Natchez, and I believe that to be a close description, although it may not be quite as vigorous or tall as Natchez.

This is certainly an outstanding National Arboretum introduction. It will quickly become a major specimen landscape tree. In addition to constant, clear, bright pink summer flowering, from early July till September, this selection has an effective, strongly sinuate, mottled, cinnamon-brown trunk coloration. Its habit or form is a tall, globose tree. Beautiful fall foliage colors are bronze to maroon.

Choctaw was selected in 1970 from a cross of (**Lagerstroemia indica** Pink Lace X **Lagerstroemia fauriei**) X **Lagerstroemia indica** Potomac. It was included in a late group of introductions in 1991. Early on this cultivar was thought to be a replacement for Potomac because of more resistance to powdery mildew.

I hesitate to give Choctaw a full endorsement, since our limited experience indicates less winter hardiness and a susceptibility to late spring frost damage. But this plant has everything else necessary for stardom: a great flower, wonderful trunk coloration,

The flower of Byers Wonderful White is often larger than a basketball.

fine habit of growth, good fall color, and excellent disease and insect resistance. In our fields, the vigorous growth just doesn't appear to slow in time to avoid damage from early frosts. In more southern environments, this one is certain to be a top-flight choice.

Fantasy

When the original distribution and evaluation of **Lagerstroemia fauriei** began in the late 1950s, a group of the seedlings was given to North Carolina State University. As the plants grew, one was clearly outstanding. Dr. J. C. Raulston, a prominent plantsman and director of the North Carolina State University Arboretum in Raleigh, North Carolina, in his registration report tells of noticing the striking plant in the 1970s. He named it Fantasy in 1982 and began informal introduction the next year by recommending growers try it.

Raulston continued, "The narrow American Elm-like, vase-shaped growth habit; excellent red bark; disease free foliage; and good display of white flowers for this species," are reasons for this crapemyrtle to become a distinct cultivar.

Dr. Michael Dirr, writer and well-known horticulturist of the University of Georgia, commented after seeing the plants at that arboretum, "I witnessed these most magnificent, multistemmed, dark red-brown barked specimens. Fantasy has outstanding bark and will make a handsome small tree."

In the arboretum in 1994, Fantasy was 55 feet tall and its trunks were six inches in diameter. At Byers Nursery Company we find that Fantasy, like all pure **Lagerstroemia fauriei**, is more difficult to propagate than most crapemyrtle. The appearance of this cultivar is greatly enhanced when it grows in full sun.

Fauriei species

When Dr. John Creech collected this species in 1957, he changed the face of the crapemyrtle world. Hybridization efforts using **Lagerstroemia fauriei** were begun by Dr. Donald Egolf, and all the new hybrid cultivars bearing American Indian names were introduced by the National Arboretum.

The original plant was found growing at about 1300 feet elevation, in a mountain forest above Kurio, Yakushima, Japan. Creech found one **Lagerstroemia** of this species, indicating that it might soon become extinct in the wild. Later, three more collections were sent to the National Arboretum from other Japanese locations.

Lagerstroemia fauriei has characteristics that reappear in the newer family members: light green, lacy leaves; small, early, white flowers; smooth, exfoliating, showy burgundy to cinnamon bark; vigorous growth habit, developing into a vase-shaped tree with outward arching limbs; 20 feet or more in ultimate height; and probably most important of all, high resistance to powdery mildew. One other attribute of **Lagerstroemia fauriei** is the exceptional viability of its seeds.

As the first group of propagules were circulated around the plant world for evaluation, individuals involved with the work began making selections. Several were originally chosen. Of those, four have survived as the best: Kiowa, Fantasy, Townhouse, and Basham's Party Pink. They are further described in this section.

90

When should a pure **Lagerstroemia fauriei** be used in a landscape? I have seen the almost indescribably beautiful displays of exfoliating bark these selected seedlings provide. They must be included in botanical gardens and horticultural demonstrations, and for preserving the history of **Lagerstroemia**. But, I also have seen the dazzling displays of flower colors of the hybrids which are missed when you only use the **fauriei**. Because of this, for most landscaping uses, a full-featured hybrid will be a better choice.

Kiowa

According to a 1994 release from the National Arboretum, Kiowa originated from a shipment of cuttings of unnamed **Lagerstroemia fauriei** received in 1968 from Dr. Y. Tachibana, Botanical Garden of Osaka, City University, Katano-Cho-Kitakawachijun, Osaka Prefecture. Dr. Donald Egolf originally selected this cultivar, and later evaluation and naming was done by Dr. Randy Johnson.

We have grown it, for evaluation only, at our nursery for several years under the name of Egolf's Favorite. This multistem small tree has been growing at Washington, DC for more than 25 years and is now about 30 feet tall and 25 feet wide. Kiowa has been uninjured by winter cold in the garden planting at the National Arboretum, a somewhat protected, but not nurtured, location.

The white flower is larger and blooms longer, beginning in late June, than any other **fauriei** currently under evaluation at the Arboretum. The exceptional, brilliant, cinnamon-brown, exfoliating bark, especially with the large caliper trunks, is the feature that makes this selection outstanding. And Kiowa continues to exfoliate with age, ensuring a fine bark display every year. Like most pure **Lagerstroemia fauriei**, Kiowa is difficult to root. In fact, my son Marc suggests it is the toughest. Observations indicate this selection is *completely* resistant to powdery mildew.

Limii species

This species of **Lagerstroemia** came to Dr. Egolf at the National Arboretum as seed from three provinces of China: Fujian, Zhejiang, and Hubei. He received these three accessions in 1980 from the Hangzhou Botanic Garden and in 1981 from the Shanghai Botanic Garden. These seed were shipped as **Lagerstroemia chekiangensis**, but Dr. Egolf always considered it as **Lagerstroemia limii**.

We have limited information about this species since all descriptions and documentation are written in Chinese. It is not listed in any of our plant reference books. The plants have been growing well in Washington, DC. We have a few in our nursery from hardwood cuttings I took from these original plants.

Limii is a very coarse-leafed, broad-growing plant with white flowers that one *might* recognize as crapemyrtle. From my observations, it does seem to be relatively hardy and mildew-resistant. Certainly it is vigorous. Although it is not a plant most would use instead of one of our fine cultivars, it does provide a new gene source. A group of seedlings, bred to include the three **Lagerstroemia** species **indica**, **fauriei**, and **limii,** is being tested at the Arboretum. In this group are some large-growing individuals from which we may get a big, new, deep-red flowering, hybrid crapemyrtle.

Miami

"Beauty is only skin deep," we are told. The lovely, dark-pink flower goes a long way to persuade one to plant this 1987 selection. Miami is a hybrid that makes me think we might have two lists from which we select the variety for a planting. The lists would be divided strictly by winter hardiness experience. In this case, Miami would appear on the less hardy list, yet once it is established and really gets going, it is a truly beautiful crapemyrtle.

This cultivar is an upright, usually multi-stemmed tree. It was selected from a complex 1972 cross of [**Lagerstroemia indica** Pink Lace X **Lagerstroemia fauriei**] X [**Lagerstroemia indica** Firebird X (**Lagerstroemia indica** X **Lagerstroemia fauriei** seedling)]. The mottled, dark chestnut-brown bark is effective as exfoliation occurs.

According to Dr. Egolf's observations, Miami ranges between highly tolerant and resistant to powdery mildew.

Fall foliage color is orange to dark russet. The flowers begin in early July and recurrent flowering will last for about 100 days. Our experience with Miami, and others of these large growing hybrids, leads me to believe that the greatest successes will be when these plants are grown in more southerly locations or without the vigor-increasing activities such as fertilizing, watering and pruning.

Miami must have some period of slowed growth before frost occurs. I make these charges about the threat of winter damage from my experience, but I must include information from a trial at the Southeast Missouri State University in Cape Girardeau, Missouri. In a planting done in 1987 and 1988, Miami is given an excellent rating and has grown to fourteen feet tall.

Reports of transplanting difficulty and a less vigorous root system have been made by some nurserymen.

Muskogee

Natchez and Muskogee, introduced in 1978, were the first hybrids with potential to be real crapemyrtle trees. Muskogee, a stocky, hardy cultivar, has been a substantial performer in southern landscapes. The abundant flowers are medium-size and light lavender in color, with the blooming period, beginning in mid-June, lasting for about 120 days. The flowers are well supported by strong branching. This gives a neat and substantial appearance to this small tree.

The exfoliating bark is a grey-tan to medium-brown tone and is not nearly as effective as the bark colors of Natchez. In the fall, as the days shorten and nights cool, the foliage becomes a mix of good reds and yellows.

Muskogee is the result of a 1964 cross of **Lagerstroemia indica** Pink Lace X **Lagerstroemia fauriei**. It is highly mildew resistant. The attractive and stately appearance of this selection is effective as a street tree or as a specimen with space to show off. Florida growers give this cultivar high marks.

Crapemyrtle, 20 Feet or More Tall

Basham's Party Pink
Crapemyrtle

Byers Standard Red
Crapemyrtle

20 Feet or More Tall

Biloxi Crapemyrtle

Byers Wonderful White Crapemyrtle

Photograph courtesy of
Fleming's Nurseries Pty. Ltd.,
Victoria, Australia.

Byers Wonderful White
Crapemyrtle

Carolina Beauty
Crapemyrtle

20 Feet or More Tall

Choctaw Crapemyrtle

Fantasy Crapemyrtle

Photograph courtesy of
Dr. J.C. Raulston,
Raleigh, North Carolina

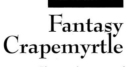

20 Feet or More Tall

Kiowa Crapemyrtle

Miami Crapemyrtle

20 Feet or More Tall

Natchez Crapemyrtle

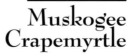

Muskogee
Crapemyrtle

Flower of untested hybrid that includes Lagerstroemia limii.

Wichita Crapemyrtle

(Photo credit to U.S. National Arboretum, Washington, DC)

Townhouse Bark Crapemyrtle

Photograph courtesy of
Dr. J.C. Raulston,
Raleigh, North Carolina

Tuscarora Crapemyrtle

Potomac Crapemyrtle

Natchez

Today, Natchez is the "crown princess" of the crapemyrtle world. No other **Lagerstroemia** cultivar, from the Arboretum work or any other source, has taken the fancy of the global gardening public as has this one. In the trial gardens of the National Arboretum, Natchez has continually been the largest and most showy of all the plantings.

The outstanding feature of a mature Natchez is the astonishing, cinnamon-brown exfoliating bark which, unlike most varieties, is spectacular throughout the year. The pure white flowers can be one foot long and are in bloom for about 110 days beginning in mid-June.

Selected from the same 1964 cross of **Lagerstroemia indica** Pink Lace X **Lagerstroemia fauriei** as Muskogee, Natchez was introduced in 1987. It is highly mildew resistant. The fall foliage color is a fine red-orange.

Every southern city has this lovely crapemyrtle now approaching the most effective size. Since it is almost common, we can also call it the most abused. Those who prune by "stump-cutting" seem to attack Natchez first. Because of its good winter hardiness and cold tolerance, it will demonstrate to all just how wonderful a crapemyrtle can be. Natchez is the "pick of the patch" for now and probably for a long, long time.

One other issue surrounding Natchez is the crapemyrtle selection circulating by the name of Sarah's Favorite. Nurseries and gardens must agree to certain rules before being selected for the privilege of receiving large groups of plants for evaluation from the National Arboretum. One of those rules absolutely precludes propagating or distributing any of the group that is not eventually selected and named by the National Arboretum staff. In fact, instructions are given for destruction of all the remaining plants after the best are chosen.

Sarah's Favorite, selection 5570E (the Arboretum's research identification number), is the single breakdown in that agreement since the program began. It was judged to be inferior to Natchez and not selected, although similar in appearance. This crapemyrtle has also appeared in some nursery lists as Hybrid White. Credit for this work, if due, should belong to the National Arboretum Shrub Breeding Program. Discredit should be assigned if necessary. A few nurserymen chose to ignore the staff decision and today continue distribution. A sad story.

For all the South, Natchez is the one.

Potomac

In the mid-1960s, when my interest in crapemyrtle was developing, Potomac landed right in the middle of my thinking. In the earliest of Dr. Egolf's work, he introduced four **Lagerstroemia indica** selections. One of them, Potomac, had a most beautiful, clear, "bubble gum" pink flower, and an upright habit of growth. It was distinctly different from the old varieties we were growing.

For several years, I chose this one as my favorite. We used it and recommended it as the best. Then we were given the hybrids from crosses with **Lagerstroemia fauriei**. In comparison with most of those, Potomac dropped from the blue-ribbon list. Although the flower of Potomac is still among the most beautiful, one attribute did not measure up. Particularly, we saw continued killing back of stems and trunks when the plants were exposed to an early warm-up, then a frost, in the spring. Often growth of Potomac begins before all other crapemyrtle, then is killed to the ground by a late (in our area, about

April tenth) frost. Yet in the deep South, this can always be a very fine and productive choice for landscape uses.

This cultivar originated in 1962 from colchicine-treated seedlings and was introduced in 1967 by the National Arboretum. The orange fall foliage is especially pretty. The flowering period begins in late June and continues for about 90 days.

Townhouse

The incredible colors in the exfoliating bark of Townhouse were a surprise to Dr. J.C. Raulston. This selection was planted on the North Carolina State Arboretum grounds as a random seedling grown from seed of **Lagerstroemia fauriei** Fantasy. Hard work brings good luck.

There was no intention to release this crapemyrtle when it was placed in the garden, but its prominent location near the entrance led to many requests from the public as well as nurserymen, and it was introduced in 1986. Townhouse has the deepest red exfoliating bark colors of all in the arboretum. The growth habit is tall and wide-spreading, wider by ten degrees than its parent, Fantasy. The white flowers, while smaller and less showy than Natchez, are better than average for the species.

Tuscarora

When Tuscarora was introduced in 1981, there was great excitement in crapemyrtle circles because of its distinctive new flower color. No other selection had been developed with the exquisite, dark-coral bloom found here. This was the first pink hybrid to be designated as a cultivar. Few new plants, at that time, had been featured on the front cover of *American Nurseryman* magazine, but Tuscarora was, in July of 1982.

Originating from a 1967 cross of **Lagerstroemia indica** X **fauriei** Basham's Party Pink X **Lagerstroemia indica** Cherokee, which means that it is one quarter **Lagerstroemia fauriei**, Tuscarora was selected in 1971 and its name was registered in 1978. The effectiveness of the flowers begins with a great display in early July and continues at a slightly lessened level for about 70 days. The mottled, light brown trunks are more effective as exfoliation begins in July and August, but is remarkable all year long. The display of bark colors becomes much more attractive with the maturity after four years of growth.

Red-tinged new leaves appear in the spring, on a graceful, vase-shaped, broad-crowned habit. Tuscarora is strongly resistant to powdery mildew. Autumn coloration ranges between orange and red. This cultivar is generally thought to be in the ten to twenty foot size range, but I place it in this largest category after seeing a group, grown closely together, that were over 25 feet high.

Norm Easey of Sarasota, Florida has called Tuscarora a magnet for aphids. He feels that other crapemyrtle placed near this cultivar are adversely affected by increased aphid attack. I have not observed this.

Susceptibility to winter damage is the one weak spot for this variety. It seems to be totally root hardy in all the usual crapemyrtle country, but we often have seen some stem and trunk damage in the coldest times. However, Tuscarora has done very well in a planting in Cape Girardeau, Missouri. Professor Charles Korns of Southeast Missouri State University gives it an excellent rating.

Like others in this size category, Tuscarora must have a slow-down period before the onset of cold weather. The crapemyrtle are certainly more winter hardy when they are grown in full sun, without growth-inducing pruning, fertilizing or watering.

Wichita

Wichita may be one of the very best cultivars in this largest-growing group of crapemyrtle. It got off to a bad start, because it is very hard to root; consequently, we were late to get a sufficient quantity for proper evaluation. After the secret for propagation was discovered, it proved to be a fine selection.

As with many hard-to-root plants, juvenility is the key. Using very early softwood cuttings is the secret to acceptable rooting percentages. Late season growth is hard to root for many varieties, and certainly for those requiring more effort.

Wichita has a fine, upright, tree-like habit of growth, and is very resistant to powdery mildew. It has proven to be more winter hardy than most of the National Arboretum hybrids.

The long, tapered, light magenta-to-lavender flowers appear in early July and recurrent flowering appears for about 110 days. The smaller stems are light grey and, as the tree matures, over three to five years, the trunks become one of Wichita's finest attributes. The late summer exfoliation will present sinuous, mottled, russet-brown to dark mahogany bark, a most striking show. And the fall foliage adds to the reddish-brown display.

Wichita has the same parents as Miami, [**Lagerstroemia indica** Pink Lace X **Lagerstroemia fauriei**] X [**Lagerstroemia indica** Firebird X (**Lagerstroemia indica** X **Lagerstroemia fauriei** seedling)], and was introduced in 1987 from a 1972 cross.

The big coarse leaves of Lagerstroemia limii are very different from the crapemyrtle we see everyday.

Sources

Affleck, Thomas. *Affleck's Southern Rural Almanac and Plantation and Garden Calendar.* p.65. Ingleside, Washington, Mississippi. 1854.

Bailey, L. H. and S. Z. Bailey, *Hortus III.* MacMillan Publishing Company. New York. 1977.

Blackwell, Cecil. "Planting and Care of Crepe Myrtle 'The Flower of 101 Days.'" Birmingham Alabama. *The Progressive Farmer*, about 1966.

Byers, Marcus David, Jr. Crapemyrtle Comparison Chart. Huntsville, Alabama: Byers Nursery Co., Inc. Golden Rule Printing, 1987, 1991, and 1996.

Chopin, David Earl. A letter and information sent to David Byers. Washington, Pennsylvania. 1995.

Creech, John H. Phone conversations and letter, Hendersonville, North Carolina. September 1996.

de Forest, Elizabeth Kellam. *The Gardens & Grounds at Mount Vernon.* The Mount Vernon Ladies' Association of the Union. Mount Vernon, Virginia. 1982.

Dirr, Michael A. *Manual of Woody Landscape Plants: Their Identification, Ornamental Characteristics, Culture, Propagation and Uses.* Stipes Publishing Company, Champaign, Illinois. 1983.

Dix, Ruth. Continuing interviews and information. National Arboretum. Washington, DC. 1994-1997.

Duke, James A. and Edward S. Ayensu. *Medicinal Plants of China.* Algonac, Michigan: Reference Publications, Inc. 1985.

Egolf, Donald R. Conversations, letters and information. 1967-90.

Egolf, Donald R. and Anne O. Andrick. *The Lagerstroemia Handbook/Checklist. A Guide to Crapemyrtle Cultivars.* American Association of Botanical Gardens and Arboreta, Inc., 1978.

Einert, A. E. and V. M. Watts. *Four New Crapemyrtles-'Centennial', 'Victor', 'Hope', 'Ozark Spring'.* Arkansas Farm Research XXII(3).1967.

Farmer, Jeff and Paul Bertrand. A speech, "Pruning Crapemyrtles at Walt Disney World." The Menninger

Fisher, Robert B. *A List of Ornamental Trees and Shrubs Noted in the Writings of George Washington.* Compiled and annotated during his tenure as Horticulturist at Mount Vernon. 1945-1979.

Flint, Harrison. *Landscape Plants for Eastern North America.* John Wiley & Sons. New York. 1983.

Flowering Tree Conference, Orlando, Florida. 1993.

Floyd, John Alex. "Pruning Makes A Difference." *Southern Living*, Birmingham, Alabama. March 1995.

Haynes, C. L. and O. M. Lindstrom. "Cooling and Warming Effects on Cold Hardiness Estimations of Three Woody Ornamental Taxa." *HortScience*, Volume 27. December 1992.

Higginbotham, Julie S. "Dr. Donald Egolf." *American Nurseryman.* Chicago, Illinois. March 1, 1991.

Hunt, William Lanier. "Crepe myrtles set Southern landscapes ablaze." *The Chapel Hill Newspaper*, Chapel Hill, North Carolina, July 28, 1991.

Hutton, Richard J. "Plant Patents, Trademarks, and Other Variety Protection Devices." International Plant Propagators' Combined Proceedings. Volume 35, p 755. 1985.

Johnson, G. Randy. "When is a dwarf crape not a dwarf crape?" *Nursery Manager*, Fort Worth Texas. September 1993

Johnson, G. Randy. Letter to David Byers. National Arboretum. Washington, DC. September 16, 1993.

Keever, Gary J. and William J. Foster. "Control of Basal Sprout Regrowth on Crapemyrtle." *Journal of Environmental Horticulture.* Volume 8. December, 1990.

Kelsey, Harland P. and William A. Dayton. *Standardized Plant Names.* Harrisburg, Pennsylvania: J. Horace McFarland Company, 1942.

Knox, Gary W., Russell F. Mizell III, and Daniel O. Chellemi. "Susceptibility of Crape Myrtle Cultivars to Crapemyrtle Aphid and Powdery Mildew." *Proceedings of the Southern Nurserymen's Association Research Conference*, Volume 37. 1992.

Knox, Gary W. "Crapemyrtles for the Deep South." *American Nurseryman*, Chicago, Illinois. June 1, 1995.

Kozlowski, Yvonne and Tom Glynn. Auburn University Libraries. Information and phone calls. 1997.

Laiche, Adolph J. "Evaluation of Crape Myrtle Selections." *Mississippi Agricultural & Forestry Experiment Station Research Report.* Volume 16, Number 6. April, 1991.

Mizell, Russell F., III, and Gary W. Knox. "Susceptibility of Crapemyrtle to the Crapemyrtle Aphid in North Florida." *Journal of Entomological Science*, Volume 28, No. 1, 1993.

Pair, John C. Letters to David Byers. Wichita Kansas. 1990.

Pair, John C. Application to the International registration of Woody Plant Cultivar Names. Washington, DC. 1994.

Raulston, J. C. Letters and information to David Byers. Raleigh, North Carolina. 1993.

Rehder, Alfred. *Manual of Cultivated Trees and Shrubs.* New York: The Macmillan Company, 1949.

Sharma, Govind C. Alabama A & M University, Huntsville, Alabama. Conversations and information. 1996-1997.

Silva, Ellen M. "Hardiness of New Crape Myrtle Cultivars." Research Abstracts for the Consumer Horticulture database. (http://www.ext.vt.edu/hort...research) April 1989.

Shadow, Donald O. Conversations and information. Shadow Nursery, Winchester, Tennessee. 1994-1996.

Sparks, Dr. Beverly. A Letter to Mr. Tim Kearns, Stone Mountain, Georgia. November 1, 1993.

Spring, Otto. A Letter to the Editor, *Southern Florist and Nurseryman*, February 19, 1982.

Stamper, Anne Andrick. Conversations and letter. Nokomis, Florida. September 1996.

Taylor, Norman. *1001 Questions Answered About Flowers.* New York: Dodd, Mead and Company, 1963.

Tidwell, Bo. *Favorite Plant for LCA.* Greenville, Georgia. 1994. University of Florida. "IPM Florida." Volume 1. on Internet at http://gnv.ifas.ufl.edu/~fairsewb/ipm. Summer 1995.

Washington, George. Letter from New York to his manager. August 1776.

Washington, George. Notes from his diary. January 19, 1785

Westcott, Cynthia. *Plant Disease Handbook.* New York: Van Nostrand Reinhold Company, 1971.

Whitcomb, Carl E. *Know It and Grow It.* Published by the Author, Stillwater, Oklahoma. 1978.

Whitcomb, Carl E. "Prairie Lace Crapemyrtle." *HortScience.* Volume 19. October, 1984.

Whitcomb, Carl E. A letter to David Byers. Stillwater, Oklahoma. September, 1995

Crapemyrtle Cultivars

Name	Color	Height	Pg.
Acoma	White	5-10 feet	61
Apalachee	lavender	10-20 feet	67
Basham's Party Pink	lavender	>20 feet	86
Baton Rouge	red	< 3 feet	59
Bayou Marie	pink/red	< 3 feet	59
BiColor	red/white	< 5 feet	59
Biloxi	pink	>30 feet	87
Bourbon Street	red	< 3 feet	59
Byers Hardy Lavender	lavender	> 20 feet	87
Byers Standard Red	red	> 20 feet	88
Byers Wonderful White	white	> 20 feet	88
Caddo	pink	5-10 feet	62
Carolina Beauty	red	> 20 feet	88
Catawba	purple	10-20 feet	68
Centennial	purple	< 5 feet	53
Centennial Spirit	red	10-20 feet	68
Cherokee	red	5-10 feet	63
Chickasaw	pink	< 2 feet	54
Chisam Fire	red	< 5 feet	59
Choctaw	pink	> 20 feet	89
Comanche	pink	10-20 feet	77
Conestoga	lavender	10-20 feet	78
Cordon Bleu	lavender	< 3 feet	59
Creole	red	< 3 feet	59
Delta Blush	pink	< 2 feet	59
Dynamite	red	10-20 feet	78
Fantasy	white	> 40 feet	90
Faurei species	white	> 20 feet	90
Hope	white	< 5 feet	55
Hopi	pink	5-10 feet	63
Houston	red	< 2 feet	59
Kiowa	white	> 20 feet	91
Lafayette	lavender	< 2 feet	59
Limii species	white	> 20 feet	91
Lipan	lavender	10-20 feet	78
Mardi Gras	purple	< 3 feet	59

Name	Color	Height	Pg.
Miami	pink	> 20 feet	92
Muskogee	lavender	> 20 feet	92
Natchez	white	> 30 feet	101
Near East	pink	10-20 feet	79
New Orleans	purple	< 2 feet	59
Osage	pink	10-20 feet	79
Ozark Spring	lavender	< 5 feet	56
Pecos	pink	5-10 feet	63
Pink Blush	pink	< 2 feet	59
Pixie White	white	< 2 feet	60
Potomac	pink	> 20 feet	101
Powhatan	purple	10-20 feet	80
Prairie Lace	pink/white	5-10 feet	64
Purple Velvet	purple	< 5 feet	60
Raspberry Sundae	pink/white	10-20 feet	80
Regal Red	red	10-20 feet	81
Royal Velvet	pink	10-20 feet	82
Sacramento	red	< 3 feet	60
Seminole	pink	10-20 feet	82
Sioux	pink	10-20 feet	82
Tonto	red	5-10 feet	65
Townhouse	white	> 20 feet	102
Tuscarora	pink	> 20 feet	102
Tuskegee	pink	10-20 feet	83
Velma's Royal Delight	magenta	< 5 feet	57
Victor	red	< 5 feet	56
Wichita	lavender	> 20 feet	103
William Toovey	red	10-20 feet	84
World's Fair	red	< 3 feet	60
Yuma	lavender	10-20 feet	85
Zuni	purple	5-10 feet	66

Crapemyrtle Cultivars by Color

Name	Color	Height	pg.
Baton Rouge	**red**	< 3 feet	59
Bourbon Street	red	< 3 feet	59
Byers Standard Red	red	> 20 feet	88
Carolina Beauty	red	> 20 feet	88
Centennial Spirit	red	10-20 feet	68
Cherokee	red	5-10 feet	63
Chisam Fire	red	< 5 feet	59
Creole	red	< 3 feet	59
Dynamite	red	10-20 feet	78
Houston	red	< 2 feet	59
Regal Red	red	10-20 feet	81
Sacramento	red	< 3 feet	60
Tonto	red	5-10 feet	65
Victor	red	< 5 feet	56
William Toovey	red	10-20 feet	84
World's Fair	red	< 3 feet	60
Acoma	**white**	5-10 feet	61
Byers Wonderful White	white	> 20 feet	88
Fantasy	white	> 40 feet	90
Faurei species	white	> 20 feet	90
Hope	white	< 5 feet	55
Kiowa	white	> 20 feet	91
Limii species	white	> 20 feet	91
Natchez	white	> 30 feet	101
Pixie White	white	< 2 feet	60
Townhouse	white	> 20 feet	102
Biloxi	**pink**	>30 feet	87
Caddo	pink	5-10 feet	62
Chickasaw	pink	< 2 feet	54
Choctaw	pink	> 20 feet	89
Comanche	pink	10-20 feet	77
Delta Blush	pink	< 2 feet	59
Hopi	pink	5-10 feet	63
Miami	pink	> 20 feet	92
Near East	pink	10-20 feet	79
Osage	pink	10-20 feet	79
Pecos	pink	5-10 feet	63
Pink Blush	pink	< 2 feet	59

Name	Color	Height	pg.
Potomac	pink	> 20 feet	101
Royal Velvet	pink	10-20 feet	82
Seminole	pink	10-20 feet	82
Sioux	pink	10-20 feet	82
Tuscarora	pink	> 20 feet	102
Tuskegee	pink	10-20 feet	83
Apalachee	**lavender**	10-20 feet	67
Basham's Party Pink	lavender	>20 feet	86
Byers Hardy Lavender	lavender	> 20 feet	87
Conestoga	lavender	10-20 feet	78
Cordon Bleu	lavender	< 3 feet	59
Lafayette	lavender	< 2 feet	59
Lipan	lavender	10-20 feet	78
Muskogee	lavender	> 20 feet	92
Ozark Spring	lavender	< 5 feet	56
Wichita	lavender	> 20 feet	103
Yuma	lavender	10-20 feet	85
Catawba	**purple**	10-20 feet	68
Centennial	purple	< 5 feet	53
Mardi Gras	purple	< 3 feet	59
New Orleans	purple	< 2 feet	59
Powhatan	purple	10-20 feet	80
Purple Velvet	purple	< 5 feet	60
Zuni	purple	5-10 feet	66
Bayou Marie	pink/red	< 3 feet	59
BiColor	red/white	< 5 feet	59
Prairie Lace	pink/white	5-10 feet	64
Raspberry Sundae	pink/white	10-20 feet	80
Velma's Royal Delight	magenta	< 5 feet	57

Crapemyrtle Cultivars by Height

Name	Color	Height	pg.
Fantasy	white	> 40 feet	90
Biloxi	pink	>30 feet	87
Natchez	white	> 30 feet	101
Basham's Party Pink	lavender	>20 feet	86
Byers Hardy Lavender	lavender	> 20 feet	87
Byers Standard Red	red	> 20 feet	88
Byers Wonderful White	white	> 20 feet	88
Carolina Beauty	red	> 20 feet	88
Choctaw	pink	> 20 feet	89
Faurei species	white	> 20 feet	90
Kiowa	white	> 20 feet	91
Limii species	white	> 20 feet	91
Miami	pink	> 20 feet	92
Muskogee	lavender	> 20 feet	92
Potomac	pink	> 20 feet	101
Townhouse	white	> 20 feet	102
Tuscarora	pink	> 20 feet	102
Wichita	lavender	> 20 feet	103
Apalachee	lavender	10-20 feet	67
Catawba	purple	10-20 feet	68
Centennial Spirit	red	10-20 feet	68
Comanche	pink	10-20 feet	77
Conestoga	lavender	10-20 feet	78
Dynamite	red	10-20 feet	78
Lipan	lavender	10-20 feet	78
Near East	pink	10-20 feet	79
Osage	pink	10-20 feet	79
Powhatan	purple	10-20 feet	80
Raspberry Sundae	pink/white	10-20 feet	80
Regal Red	red	10-20 feet	81
Royal Velvet	pink	10-20 feet	82
Seminole	pink	10-20 feet	82
Sioux	pink	10-20 feet	82
Tuskegee	pink	10-20 feet	83
William Toovey	red	10-20 feet	84
Yuma	lavender	10-20 feet	85
Acoma	White	5-10 feet	61
Caddo	pink	5-10 feet	62
Cherokee	red	5-10 feet	63

Name	Color	Height	pg.
Hopi	pink	5-10 feet	63
Pecos	pink	5-10 feet	63
Prairie Lace	pink/white	5-10 feet	64
Tonto	red	5-10 feet	65
Zuni	purple	5-10 feet	66
BiColor	red/white	< 5 feet	59
Chisam Fire	red	< 5 feet	59
Hope	white	< 5 feet	55
Ozark Spring	lavender	< 5 feet	56
Purple Velvet	purple	< 5 feet	60
Velma's Royal Delight	magenta	< 5 feet	57
Victor	red	< 5 feet	56
Baton Rouge	red	< 3 feet	59
Bayou Marie	pink/red	< 3 feet	59
Bourbon Street	red	< 3 feet	59
Cordon Bleu	lavender	< 3 feet	59
Creole	red	< 3 feet	59
Mardi Gras	purple	< 3 feet	59
Sacramento	red	< 3 feet	60
World's Fair	red	< 3 feet	60
Chickasaw	pink	< 2 feet	54
Delta Blush	pink	< 2 feet	59
Houston	red	< 2 feet	59
Lafayette	lavender	< 2 feet	59
New Orleans	purple	< 2 feet	59
Pink Blush	pink	< 2 feet	59
Pixie White	white	< 2 feet	60

David Byers is a third-generation nurseryman. He has always been in a horticulture business. Since he graduated from Alabama Polytechnic Institute, now Auburn University, he has sold crapemyrtle across America and around the world. He writes and speaks about his favorite plant for many audiences and now has compiled, as he calls it, "More than anyone wants to know about crapemyrtle."

Byers has served with the leadership in nursery associations and received several awards for his work from the horticultural industry.

He knows many who have labored with crapemyrtle and these special relationships give him insights unavailable to most. He and wife Janie live in Huntsville, Alabama. They have three sons and two granddaughters.

He can be reached at P.O. Box 434, Huntsville, AL 35804.

E-mail byersdavid@AOL.com